THE
JENNY CRUMB

Martina Dalton

WRITE AS RAIN BOOKS

Martina Dalton

Cover Design by Martina Dalton
Cover Model, Madeline Dalton
Photo by Tammy Davison

First Edition, 2014
ISBN 978-1502726827

Dedication

This book is dedicated to my beautiful sister, Marion, who left this earth too soon. She was my steadfast supporter and my lifelong friend. I was blessed to have shared my childhood with her.

Acknowledgements

My second novel, *The Sixth Sense of Jenny Crumb*, was a joy to write. I'd like to thank my sister, Marion, to whom this book is dedicated. She was my cheerleader and ardent encourager. She passed away before this book was published, but I'm sure she was allowed an advance copy to peruse in heaven. I love you, sis.

Secondly, I'd like to thank my family, Matt, Madeline, and Kai. I am grateful to have them cheering me on in the wings. Thanks and hugs go to my mom, Lindy Sutter—I don't know what I'd do without her.

My heartfelt thanks goes out to my wonderful writing critique group, *Writers in the Rain*. My book is so much better due to their vigilant critiques. Thank you, Angela Orlowski-Peart, Fabio Bueno, Eileen Riccio, Brenda Beem, and Suma Subramaniam from the bottom of my heart.

I also wanted to extend a thank you to my wonderful and talented editor, Alyssa Palmer. Thanks to my friend, Tammy Davison of Bella Photography, who took the beautiful photo for the cover. Thanks also to the real-life psychics Char Sundust and Pamela Jensen. These two ladies are immensely gifted and were so generous with their time. Special thanks go to beta readers Douglas Gray and Sharon McIndoo.

And last, but not least, thanks to my knowledgeable boating friends, Mike Finn and Rick Sunde who helped me pick the right type of boat for Jenny and her family to travel to Alaska on. Their nautical expertise was essential in making the story more realistic. Rick also passed away this year, so I send much love to his family and gigantic circle of friends.

Chapter 1

I used to think of being psychic as a curse, but I've come to believe that it's a gift. After all, I saved a girl's life and perhaps the lives of other girls who might have been murdered if the creepy guy had not been killed. During the last half of my junior year in high school, I survived a nasty fall off the top of a cheerleading pyramid, recovered from a concussion, and helped save a girl from a kidnapper.

Now that the drama was over, I was determined to have a nice, quiet summer.

It was warm and sunny. A light breeze ruffled my hair, and I breathed in a deep whiff of lilac-scented air. I took the keys out of my pocket and unlocked my car.

I couldn't wait to see Mike, who was at his home recovering from a knife injury. He had nearly been killed when my would-be kidnapper, Richard Grist, stuck a knife in his chest and tried to abduct me. Needless to say, I was over-the-moon grateful that Mike had survived, and that he still wanted a relationship with me, despite the danger.

I started my car and drove up Forest Drive, heading toward Mike's house.

Suddenly, a crow flew right over my windshield, its wings grazing the glass and startling me. I jerked the wheel to the right and nearly hit a hedge.

"Whoa!" I quickly corrected my direction, my heart pounding wildly.

Where did that bird come from? Crows were usually very smart and were rarely hit by cars. What was up with that one? I took a couple of deep breaths and continued on.

Mike lived at the top of Cougar Mountain, up a narrow wooded road. I drove around the circular drive and parked my car in one of the four spots available. The house was a large Craftsman-style structure. The big timber beams accented with river rock made it seem like a woodsy lodge or hotel instead of an ordinary home. It looked like something right out of the pages of Architectural Digest. I walked up the cobblestone drive lined with huckleberry bushes and stepped up to the massive wooden door to ring the bell.

A burst of barking sounded on the other side of the door. Mike's overgrown four-month old Alaskan Malamute puppy, Kaya, could sure be intimidating when she wanted to be. I smiled, thinking how ferocious the fluffball sounded.

I heard footsteps hurrying to the door and then, "Kaya! Tone it down, girl. It's just Jenny."

The door opened and Mike bent over, grunting as he scooped up Kaya and stepped back from the door to let me in.

"Ugh. She weighs a ton already." He grimaced and stroked her neck.

"I thought you weren't supposed to pick up anything heavy." I nudged him. "She must weigh at least forty-five pounds by now."

He smiled, closed the door behind me, and gave me a one-armed hug and a quick kiss. Kaya smooshed between us and began licking my chin.

"Well, I thought I'd pick her up before she grows anymore."

I grabbed her little muzzle. "Oh Kaya, you are a sassy little thing." I kissed her head and patted her soft, fluffy neck.

Kaya's tail wagged furiously, causing her back end to wiggle back and forth. Mike set her down and she pounced on me, licking my bare ankles. I sat down on the floor and let her crawl all over me.

"You know, I'm surprised your parents let you get a dog, what with all their moving from place to place." I scratched the puppy behind her ears.

"I was surprised too. But after I had that talk with them about how important it was for me to settle down in one place for a while, they seemed to really take that to heart. I think they plan on staying here for at least a year, maybe even more. We'll see." He knelt down beside me and kissed me.

Again, Kaya pushed her way in between us, licking our faces.

"You're quite the chaperone, girl." Mike picked up the squirmy puppy and scratched her behind the ears.

"So, what's the plan for today?" he asked.

"I think we should pick up some food for a picnic. How 'bout if we drive over to West Seattle and have lunch on the beach?"

"Sounds great. I've never been to the beach here."

I giggled. "The beaches in Washington are a little bit different than the ones you're used to in California. There are a lot more rocks than sand."

"I didn't really live there long enough to get well acquainted with the beaches," he said.

"I'm sure that you'll like the one at Lincoln Park, though. The ferry terminal is there and we can watch them sail in from Vashon Island."

An hour later, we were at the seashore with a full spread of delicious food laid out on the log we were sitting on. My pesto mozzarella Panini sandwich was still warm and practically melted in my mouth. Mike seemed to be thoroughly enjoying his turkey sandwich, which he devoured in less than five minutes. While we munched on our chips, we watched a ferry coming in.

The waves gently gurgled on the rocks a few yards away, putting me into a zen-like mood. I filled my lungs with the briny air, and let myself relax.

"You're right," Mike said, breaking the silence. "This is definitely not like California. It's so much better!"

"Really?" I gave him a curious look. "What about the beautiful sand? And the tan California babes playing volleyball in bikinis?" I teased.

"Who needs that when I have my very own beach babe?" His eyes sparkled.

"Who, me?" I answered, batting my eyelashes.

"Yes, you." He leaned over and kissed me gently. My insides melted. He always had that effect on me.

Our kiss deepened, until I caught movement out of the corner of my eye.

A crow flew by, circled once, and then landed on a nearby log.

"Looks like someone wants to share our lunch," Mike said.

I picked up one of my chips and threw it in the direction of the crow. It was too light to go very far and dropped just a few feet away from us. I was just about to throw another one— farther this time, when the crow flew to the chip, surprising me with its boldness.

The black bird looked directly at me—a penetrating stare that seemed to bore a hole straight through me. It held my gaze for several seconds, then snatched the treat and flew back to the log.

"Wow." I swallowed hard. "That was strange. He wasn't scared of me at all."

"People probably feed them all the time here," Mike said. "He must be used to getting handouts."

The crow called out, his eyes never leaving mine. A second bird landed on a log on the opposite side of the first crow.

"Guess he's calling his friends over for the party." Mike smiled. "Who can resist a good potato chip?"

But then, a third and fourth crow landed behind us, followed by three more. Mike and I exchanged an uneasy glance. I couldn't decide whether or not this was really cool or kind of scary.

More and more crows were arriving, making a black semi-circle around us.

"What... what should we do?" I stammered, turning around to see dozens of the shiny black birds.

"I have no idea."

I turned and looked directly at the first crow. "What is it? Are you trying to tell us something?"

The bird let out an abrupt caw, and suddenly, the entire murder of crows took to the air, their wings flapping noisily over our heads as they headed north along the beach.

Mike shook his head. "Weird."

"Yeah." I watched the crows grow smaller as they continued flying away.

I wondered if they really *were* trying to tell me something. But what? Perhaps it was just a strange occurrence. Strange things happened all the time. However, over the course of the year, I had learned a thing or two about psychic premonitions. Sometimes, those little things that we noticed really *did* mean something. And if we weren't paying attention, we'd miss an important piece of information—a clue for what was to come.

"Mike," I said, biting my lip, "something like this happened on my way to your house."

"Really? What?"

"A crow flew right across my windshield as I was driving. I nearly drove off the road."

"That *is* strange, but maybe it's just a coincidence."

"Maybe. I just hope something bad isn't about to happen."

"You and me both," Mike said, his fingers unconsciously fluttering to the knife wound on his chest.

We packed up our garbage and headed toward the paved path that ran along the beach. Kids zoomed past us on their bicycles and joggers speckled the trail ahead of us.

"Oh, I forgot to mention," Mike said as he put his arm around me, "I'm going to the San Juan Islands with my family next week."

"What?" I stopped in my tracks.

"It's just for six or seven days, though."

"Why didn't you tell me?" I put my hands on my hips.

Mike laughed at my pouting. "Because my parents didn't tell me until this morning!"

"Couldn't they have given you a little more notice?"

"Well, apparently my dad's boss invited us on the spur of the moment. They thought it would be fun to get away so they jumped at the opportunity." He reached out and put his hands on my shoulders. "Are you angry with me?"

"No. I guess I was just looking forward to spending more time with you, that's all. I'm being selfish."

"You're not selfish. I like a girl who wants to be with me. We'll spend lots of time together when I come back. Don't worry."

I wrapped my arms around his neck and kissed him. We had the whole summer to be together.

Chapter 2

The next day brought overcast skies and the smell of rain. I peeked out the window, hoping for sun. Maybe the clouds would burn off, and it would clear up later. I got up and padded downstairs to the kitchen.

Mom stood at the stove, flipping pancakes.

"Good morning!" she said brightly. "Would you mind cutting up some cantaloupe, Jenny?"

"No problem," I said, grabbing a knife out of the wooden block next to the coffee maker. I got out a cutting board and washed the melon quickly in the sink. I dried it off, thunked it down on the board, and began slicing it.

"Plans for the day?" she asked.

"Mike and I are going to hang out. We want to spend as much time together as we can because next week he and his parents are going to the San Juan Islands."

"Well, don't forget about your other friends. I'm sure they'd like to see you too."

I pushed the hair out of my face and tucked it behind my ears. "Hannah and her family went to Canada. And Julia and Aya went to a cheerleading camp in California."

"What about your theatre friend, Madeline?" Mom asked.

I put the last slice of cantaloupe in the bowl. "She's spending time with Callie. She thought she almost lost her best friend to the kidnapper, remember?"

I'd met Madeline when I auditioned for the school musical. Her dad just happened to be a detective. He was the one I had worked with to find the missing girl, Callie Shoemaker.

Mom nodded apologetically. "Of course, you're right. I just don't want you getting too serious with Mike, I guess. You're young and have your whole future ahead of you."

"Oh, come on. This is my first real boyfriend. We're taking it slow—you can trust me, right?"

She sighed. "Yes, I trust you. I just remember what it was like to be that age and to really care about someone. Sometimes, it can take over your life without you realizing it."

My phone rang, jolting us out of our conversation.

"Maybe that's Mike." I ran to pick it up. "Hello?" I said, breathlessly.

"Hi, Jenny." The woman sounded familiar, but I couldn't place who she was.

"Yes?" I answered.

"Jenny, it's Celine."

"Oh, Celine! It's so nice to hear from you."

Celine was the woman who helped me when I needed to control my abilities. She was a very talented psychic and even ran her own school to help people develop their skills.

"I'm calling because I have a few spots open in my summer camp," she said brightly. "I thought you might enjoy joining our group."

"Summer camp?" I asked, wondering what on earth she could be talking about. A psychic summer camp?

"It's really more like a summer intensive course. I'll be teaching students to better control their gifts. We'll be

8

working on getting comfortable with our abilities and channeling them more effectively."

"Sounds like it would be good for me. When does it start?"

"Next week," Celine answered. "It runs Monday through Friday."

I wrote down the details and cleared it with Mom. This was an interesting turn of events. I was excited, but a little hesitant. I was getting used to being different and there were some things that I really loved about it. But there was still a part of me that was hanging on to wanting a more "normal" life.

***

I went to bed late. I yawned as I pulled on my pajamas and sank down into my soft bed. I was thinking of Mike and what my mom had said about relationships taking over your life without you even realizing it. Would that be so bad? Feeling this way about someone was wonderful—and right now I felt like I was at the threshold of a fabulous adventure waiting to unfold. I pulled my covers up to my chin and turned off my lamp.

I was on a boat, rocking gently on a dark ocean—the sky black, except for the luminescent moon. I was mesmerized by the light dancing on the glistening water.

A sharp pain in my head caught me off balance, and I toppled headlong into the salty spray. Orange light shone through my closed eyelids as I heard a woman's screams.

I woke with a start, taking in short gasping breaths. A dream. I had come to know dreams like this one, and it was a bad sign; a very bad sign that something awful was going to happen. Then again, maybe it didn't mean anything at all. Not every dream was an omen.

I shivered and rolled over onto my side, pulling my blankets up to my chin. I hoped it had nothing to do with Mike and his upcoming boat trip. I fell back into an uneasy sleep.

***

The next morning, I quickly showered and got ready for the day. I fixed myself a bowl of cereal with milk and a sliced banana and sat down at the kitchen table.

Aside from the crunching of my cereal, the house was quiet. Almost too quiet, I thought as I got up to turn on the little television on the kitchen counter. My parents were working and Jackson was at camp. Lucky for me, the little twerp had day camp for the next two weeks, and I'd have some peace and quiet in the mornings.

The local news was on, and they were just finishing up with the weather report. It looked like the weather was clearing up—blue skies for at least another five days.

"Police and search parties are still searching for five-year-old Devon McLeod after he was reported missing by his mother, Louise Draker," the anchor said as a picture of a boy appeared on the screen.

"According to police, the boy has been missing since yesterday morning. He was last seen playing on the playground near his home in Renton."

Flash.

The boy went down the slide and stopped at the bottom, riveted to the motion in the bushes beyond. A tall man emerged from the brush, reaching out his arms to the boy.

I shook my head, trying to clear the image. Oh my God. The boy. I had to do something.

I ran up to my room and grabbed my cell phone. I needed to talk to Madeline's dad. I quickly called him.

"Detective Coalfield," his deep voice answered.

10

"Detective! It's Jenny."

"Everything all right?"

"I'm fine, but, I just got an image of the little boy who is missing. The boy from Renton. I just saw him on the news."

"Devon McLeod?" he asked.

"Yeah, that's him."

"What did you see?"

I described the scene at the playground.

"Okay, can you describe the man?"

I thought for a second. What did he look like? "Uh... tall, I think. Brown hair—I didn't get much detail." I now regretted my decision to call. I knew that I hardly had any information for him to go on.

"Anything else?"

"No. I'm sorry. It was probably stupid of me to call." My shoulders slumped.

"No, it wasn't stupid. But you probably know that I can't do much with that."

"Yeah, I'm sorry."

"Don't be sorry. If you get any more information, even if it's a little thing, go ahead and call. Every bit counts."

"Detective, how is Madeline? What is she doing this summer? I haven't seen her since the last day of school."

"Oh, she's doing really well. She and Callie are rehearsing for a play at Youth Theatre Northwest. It's over on Mercer Island."

"Really? I'd love to go see it."

"I'll have her contact you to give you the dates the show is running."

"Thanks. I'll call you if I get any more details on the little boy."

He thanked me and hung up. A play... why didn't I think of that? I should have auditioned for something as well. At least I had Celine's class to look forward to... and a few more days with Mike before he left for the San Juans.

***

This time, Mike picked me up at my house after lunch. The sun had burned away the clouds, just as I had hoped. We walked to his car—a new BMW—a graduation present from his parents. I smiled, touching the shiny black exterior. His dad's government job must pay extremely well. He opened the car door for me, and I slipped inside. The leather seats were warm from the sun. It had that new car smell that I loved.

"Where are we going?" I asked.

He closed his door and started the engine. "How does Snoqualmie Falls sound?"

"Sounds good." I was grateful that I had worn my running shoes and jeans.

"Have you ever been there?" Mike asked as we drove down Forest Drive to the freeway.

"I think when I was a little kid," I answered. "I just have a vague memory—I don't remember much except that the waterfall was really loud."

He laughed. "Well, hopefully it will be a little quieter today."

***

We got out of the car and walked up the trail toward the Falls, taking our time as we picked a few blueberries along the way. Visitors lingered, taking photos at every vantage.

The main lookout area was on a cliff, a hundred yards from the parking lot. We stopped at the chain link fence and took in the spectacular sight.

"Wow," we both uttered simultaneously, and then laughed.

The water cascaded over the top of the cliff, crashing below, white foam billowing around the base. The misty spray sparkled like a million tiny diamonds as it floated up into the atmosphere. A rainbow appeared in the mist, taking our breath away.

"This is really beautiful." Mike pulled me closer.

"It's amazing... and even more amazing because I'm with you."

He turned me toward him and gently tilted my chin up to kiss me. The sound of the waterfall melted away, and the world was only Mike.

He took me in his arms and whispered, "I wouldn't trade this moment for anything."

Looking into his green eyes, I couldn't have agreed more.

We kissed again. Suddenly, the sound of the waterfall became louder—roaring in my head. I pulled away from Mike, holding my hands over my ears.

Flash.

The water was so cold, chilling me to the bone, I gasped as I came up for air. The orange light coming from the boat nearly blinded me. An explosion ripped through the night, sending big chunks of debris flying. The last thing I saw was something jagged coming straight at me. I sank down into the blackness, watching the dancing lights above me on the surface.

"Jenny!" Mike shouted.

I was trembling and dizzy.

"I... I need to sit down," I sputtered.

"Okay, here—let's go sit down on the bench." He led me to the wooden bench not far from the fence. I sat down and bent over, my hands cradling my head on my knees.

"Are you all right?" He rubbed my back. "What happened?"

13

"I don't know. I saw something. A vision, I guess. I was in the water. It was so cold. Then the boat blew up, and something hit me on the head."

"A boat?" he asked, looking puzzled.

"It was on fire." I frowned.

He looked at me with concern. His hand automatically rested on my forehead. "You don't feel hot. I thought maybe..." his voice trailed off.

"No, I'm not sick, Mike." I sat up straight and turned to him. "I don't know what that was, but I'm hoping you'll be all right on your boat trip next week."

He looked slightly alarmed. "You think that was a vision? Does it have something to do with my upcoming vacation?"

"I don't know. I hope not," I said, searching his face for reassurance. "All I know is that it's the second vision I've had today."

I explained about the first one—the one where I had been standing on a boat and felt a blow to my head, toppling me over the side.

"So, let me see if I understand this," he said. "When you see these images, are you seeing them through the eyes of someone else?"

"Yes, that's how it has worked in the past, anyway."

"Do you know who you are within the vision? Like who it's happening to?" he asked.

I shook my head. "No, I can't see that. Maybe if the person were standing near a mirror, then maybe I could see them in the reflection. But that's never happened. I don't know who the person on the boat is."

He took a deep breath. "Wow."

"Yeah, wow. I'm sorry—I didn't mean to scare you. Maybe this happened to a person I don't even know. I don't understand why I would be having premonitions about someone I can't help. It's all a mystery to me."

14

Mike was quiet for a moment and then said, "Well, I'll just be extra careful on the boat trip. I'll wear a life jacket at all times and a buoy on my head."

I grinned and elbowed him. "Okay, wise guy! Maybe you should wear water wings too."

He laughed, pulling me off the bench. "Come on, let's go and see if we can find a place to have a cup of coffee."

Chapter 3

The next day was a Saturday—two days before Mike had to leave for his boat trip. I paced at home all morning, worrying about him. What if the visions I was having about the explosion on the boat were about Mike? I tried to remember all of the details, but they started jumbling together in my mind.

Not knowing how to decipher it all, I went downstairs to the kitchen and grabbed a notepad and pen lying next to the phone.

I jotted down, "Boat Vision: What I Know." Beneath that, I wrote:

Night
Calm water
Full moon
Something hit person on the head
Fell into the water
Fire
Explosion
Woman screaming on the boat
Debris hit person in the water
Person drowned?

That didn't tell me anything about the person that this was happening to. I tried scanning my memory again. Did I look at my clothes as I fell into the water? No… it was too dark. Did I hear myself scream? No.

I sighed in frustration and slammed the pen down on the table.

Just then, Mom walked in.

"What's wrong?"

I shook my head and puffed out a breath of air. "I can't figure this out."

I explained my latest dreams and visions. Amazing how just a month ago, I had desperately tried to keep my psychic ability from her. Now, here I was, spilling my secrets almost casually.

Mom sat down heavily in a kitchen chair. "That is really scary. Have you told Mike about this?"

"Yup. He said he'd be extra careful on the boat. I don't know what else to do."

"Maybe these visions have nothing to do with Mike. Maybe this is about a person you will never know. Or about something that has already happened."

I frowned. "I don't know, but it's really disturbing. I don't think I'd be seeing all of this if there wasn't some sort of connection to me."

The phone rang, making my heart skip a beat.

"I'll get it!" Dad called from the family room.

"Anyway," Mom said, "if it does have anything to do with you or someone you know, you're not going to find out right away. It's better not to get too upset about it— you'll just make yourself crazy with worry."

"I wish it were that easy. I know that I shouldn't be obsessed, but I can't help thinking about it."

Jackson sauntered into the kitchen. "What's for breakfast, Mom?"

"What would you like?" she asked.

"Bacon and donuts."

"Ugh, Jackson! You'll never make it to forty," I said with a grimace.

He stuck his tongue out at me. "Why do you care?"

I rolled my eyes. Yeah, why did I care? "Whatever."

Mom tried her best to put her patient face on. "Jackson, I don't have any donuts. How 'bout bacon, eggs, and fruit?"

"Fruit? That's not a breakfast item," he said with disgust.

I groaned, got up, and grabbed my notepad and pen. I was just about to leave the kitchen when Dad came in.

"You'll never guess who that phone call was from." A big grin was spread across his face.

"Who?" Mom asked.

"From Callie Shoemaker's dad, Jim. He said he wanted to do something special for us because Jenny here saved Callie's life." He clapped me on the shoulder.

"Really?" Mom got the bacon out of the refrigerator. "What did he say?"

"Is he sending us to Disneyland?" Jackson asked hopefully.

"Nope... something even better." Dad's eyes twinkled.

"Better than Disneyland?" Jackson asked. "How is that possible?"

Dad paused a moment, letting the anticipation build.

"Jim is letting us stay at their vacation home in Sitka, Alaska! And get this... he owns a boat dealership in Seattle. He's taking a boat up to Alaska for a customer, and he wanted to know if we would like to tag along. If we like the boat and the trip, he'll sell us a boat just like it... at *cost!*"

Jackson plunked himself down on a kitchen chair, clearly disappointed.

Mom and I exchanged a nervous glance.

Oh crap. A boat.

Chapter 4

"Dad, you're not seriously considering this, are you?"

"Considering? Yeah. I have, and we're doing this," he said. "Come on! It will be good for us. We'll have lots of family time. It'll be an adventure."

Mom looked a little pale. I could tell she was shocked and starting to get a little annoyed.

"When? When are we going? Next summer?" I asked.

"No." He was giddy. "This summer. I think we can take off in about a week—I've got loads of planning to do. Lucky for us, Jim's made the trip dozens of times and he really knows what he's doing."

"A week? Wait, what? We haven't even discussed this yet. What about work? I can't just take off at a moment's notice." My mother was agitated.

"Mary, I have it all under control." Dad put his arm around her. "I'm going to call your boss right now and get this all ironed out."

"What?" Mom pulled away from him. "Are you out of your mind?"

Dad laughed. "Sometimes, I can be a little crazy. But right now, I'm definitely sane. This is an opportunity of a lifetime. The kids are getting older. Pretty soon they'll be off living their own lives. Why not do this while we still have the chance?"

My mom's face lost its hardened resolve. I could tell Dad's argument was starting to wear her down.

She took him by the elbow. "At least—let's, uh, discuss this in private, okay?"

Oh, my God. He was totally going to convince her to do this.

"But what about Mike?" I stammered. "I wanted to spend the rest of the summer with him!"

"Oh, you'll have plenty of time with Mike." Dad waved me off. "He's going to the University of Washington, for God's sake. It's not like he's going off to Oxford or somewhere else far away."

He obviously didn't understand. Once Mike went to the UW—or U-Dub as most Seattleites called it, he'd be in a different world: the college world. Late nights studying, parties... He might as well be a thousand miles away. High school would seem like a closed chapter in his life. And possibly, he would be attracted to college girls and forget all about me. I wanted to spend the rest of the summer making our bond stronger.

"But, Dad! I really want to just be here this summer." I knew I had to pull this one last card to get him to change his mind. "After all I've been through this school year, I just want to stay here at home where it's safe."

My dad's expression softened. He pulled me into a hug. "I'm sorry, princess, I know you've been through a lot. But I do think this is the right thing to do. You'll be safe with your family... on a really cool boat."

Safe?

"Dad, I need to tell you something," I motioned for him to sit down at the table. I explained my dreams to him. My fingers trembled as I twisted a lock of hair. "So, you see why I don't think we should get on a boat? It would be reckless."

Dad sat and mulled things over. "I see why you would be scared, Jenny. But I don't think that your dream is about us. If it were, you'd probably have more details, and there don't seem to be many details in your dream."

Ugh, again with the details. First the missing boy on the news, and not enough specifics to help find him, and now this.

"I just think maybe we should consider the danger before we—"

"Jenny!" Dad cut me off. "It's going to be *fine*. I'll make sure that nothing happens to you. I promise."

I looked at Jackson for some help. He yawned. Couldn't the little twerp be on my side just this once?

Damn. Dad was too jazzed about this to give in. We were going on this boat trip whether we liked it or not.

How was I going to tell Mike that our perfect summer together had just come to an abrupt end?

Chapter 5

I pulled the curtain aside and looked out the window.

"He's here." I grabbed my cell phone and shoved it into the front pocket of my jeans.

"Have a good time, honey," Mom called from the kitchen. "What time will you be back?"

"I don't know, maybe around six o'clock or so. Mike has to pack for his trip, so he can't stay out late. We're just going to go for a walk around Green Lake."

"So, you'll be home for dinner then?"

"Yup. Bye, Mom!"

I ran out the front door. Mike was just getting out of his car when he caught my eye and smiled. He walked around to the passenger side and opened the door for me.

"Hi there." He leaned in to kiss me. "You look like you're in a hurry to get out of there."

I glanced back at my house.

"Yeah, I guess so." I slipped into the seat.

Mike went around the car, opened his door, and got in.

"Did you have a fight with your parents or something?"

"No, not really." I ran my fingers through my hair. "It's a long story. I'll tell you on the way to Green Lake."

***

I told Mike the whole thing—starting with my frustration at not being able to figure out who my visions were about, and ending with my dad's crazy idea to take a boat up to Sitka.

Mike shook his head. "I can't believe he would just spring that on you."

"Oh, I know. Even after I told him that I just wanted to spend a nice summer here. After the hell I've been through earlier this year, you'd think he would be somewhat sympathetic."

"Well, it sounds like he is really set on having this family adventure, as you call it. I get that. But I'm kind of upset that I don't get to hang out with you."

I swallowed the lump in my throat and blinked back the tears.

"That's all I really wanted," I answered.

He reached over and patted my knee. "It'll be all right."

I could feel he was struggling with his emotions, just like I was.

I bit my lip. "Mike—I'm worried about us."

His eyebrows furrowed, and he glanced at me quickly while trying to keep his eye on the road. "What do you mean?"

"I'm scared that when you go to college, you'll get so wrapped up in your life there, that…"

"That I'll forget about you?" he asked.

I nodded.

"Jenny, that's ridiculous!" He reached for my hand and squeezed it. "How could I forget about you? You're my first true…"

I turned to him, my eyes widened in surprise. Was he going to say, *love*? My heart skipped a beat.

"Uh, my first real girlfriend," he stammered. "You don't just forget about the first girl who captures your heart."

I blinked. My mind was racing. Had he been going to say that he loved me? Because I think I could love him—or just really, really like him. This was so confusing. My head and heart were spinning with different scenarios and possibilities. My head was saying that seventeen was way too young to pronounce your love for someone else. I mean, there was my senior year of high school and then college to think about. I really shouldn't *love* anyone right now. But my heart, thumping loudly in my chest was saying something else.

I turned toward him. "Mike, do you think that how you feel about someone—do you think that it could get in the way of what they *should* do? Like school or whatever?"

God, why was I being so practical about this? I wished I hadn't said that.

He frowned. "Are you saying that we shouldn't feel... strongly about each other?"

I shook my head. "No, no, that's not what I'm saying. I really, really want to have time with you. To see where this goes."

Silence. I waited a moment.

Did I blow it?

He nodded slowly. "I think I know what you're saying."

He left it at that. But I wasn't sure what he meant.

***

We found a parking spot on a residential street near the lake and got out of the car. A warm breeze tugged at my long hair; a blonde strand stuck itself onto my lip gloss. I pulled it away and held out my hand to Mike. He hesitated a moment, and then reached his hand out to mine.

"Mike?"

"Yeah?"

"Are you angry with me?"

He said nothing as we made our way to the sidewalk that skirted the lake. "No," he finally said.

"Really?"

"Okay, yes, I am a little upset by what you said."

"I'm so sorry," I blurted out. "I don't know why I said that. It came out all wrong. It's just that—I don't want to lose you to someone else at college. But then again, I don't want you to do poorly at school because I'm distracting you. Oh, I don't know *what* I'm saying."

Mike looked puzzled. And I completely understood why he was confused, because I didn't know what I was trying to say either.

He stopped walking and turned to me. "So, let me see if I'm getting this right. You are afraid I'll meet another girl at school, but you don't want to go out with me because you're afraid you might distract me from my studies?"

"Yes! I mean, no!"

"What?"

"Ugh. Yes, I mean I'm afraid you'll fall for another girl at the U-Dub. And no, I don't want to *not* see you. You're all I can think about. I want to go out with you—I just don't want to keep you from doing well in school. Did that come out right?"

Mike paused and then burst out laughing.

"What's so funny?"

"You are!" he said, pulling me close and hugging me. "You are completely and utterly confusing."

Now it was my turn to be confused. "You find that endearing in some way?"

"Yeah." He grinned. "You're kind of cute when you're all worried."

"Uh, thanks. I think." I wondered how I could go from a girl who had it pretty much together to a complete basket case in just a few days. What was wrong with me?

Mike grabbed my hand. "Come on, let's just walk and enjoy the afternoon."

Chapter 6

When I woke up the next morning, the TV was on in the family room, but no one was watching it. Stupid Jackson. Why couldn't he just be responsible and turn it off when he was done? I picked up the remote from the coffee table and was about to click the power button, when I noticed that it wasn't on a kids' channel; it was on a local news station.

"Authorities still have no leads on the whereabouts of the missing boy, Devon McLeod. The boy was last seen on Thursday, playing at a park near his home in Renton. Police ask that if you have any information regarding this case, to please call 911."

The picture of the little boy flashed on the screen—his dark eyes and bright smile, so innocent, in light of his current situation.

As I studied his face, the room faded away.

Flash.

The man emerged out of the bushes and reached his arms out. The boy hesitated for a moment and then walked toward the man.

Panic bubbled up from my chest to my throat as my hands reached out to steady myself on the back of the couch. I stood there and forced myself to stay within the vision. I needed to see what the man looked like.

Through the boy's eyes, I studied the man's face. Caucasian with dark hair and dark eyes. Maybe Italian? His straight hair was collar length.

He touched my face. "Dev? It's been so long... I've missed you."

Oh my God! This guy knew the boy—and now I had a description for the detective.

I ran into the kitchen where I had left my phone, and keyed in Detective Coalfield's number.

"Detective Coalfield," he answered.

"It's Jenny."

"Hi, Jenny. What's going on?"

"It's about the missing boy, Devon. He knew the man who took him!"

"Wow! Okay, that's good. Anything else? A description or location?" he asked.

"I don't have a location, but I can tell you what he looks like." I described the man in detail and then told the detective what he had said to Devon.

"Huh," he grunted. "Interesting."

"What? Does he match anyone you've been suspecting?"

"I'd have to check into that, but your description kind of matches Devon himself."

I thought for a moment. "Maybe someone related to Devon?"

"Perhaps."

"That seems like kind of a long shot. I mean, there are thousands—no millions of men who match that description." I started to lose hope.

"Yeah," he answered. "But if he knows Devon, then I'd bet it was someone Devon was related to."

"Like his dad?" I asked.

"Possibly. But we've already interviewed Vince McLeod thoroughly. He was out of town at the time Devon disappeared."

I chewed on my lip, thinking of all the possibilities. "An uncle maybe?"

"I'll check," he said. "Tell you what, if you come up with any other details, let me know. But this is good information, Jenny, really good. I need to get on this right away. Give me a call if you think of anything else, okay?"

"Sure," I said.

"And Jenny," he added.

"Yeah?"

"Thanks."

"You're welcome. Bye, Detective."

I hung up and sat down at the table. I shook my head, and tried to conjure up any other details I had seen in my vision. Why couldn't I just see more? It was so frustrating. I wanted to just *know* who took Devon and where to find him. Trying to extract the information from my visions bit by bit was like pulling teeth.

That poor little boy. What if whoever took him had hurt him? Or worse. I couldn't bring myself to imagine it.

The phone rang, jolting me out of my thoughts.

I jumped up to answer it. "Hello?"

"Hey, babe."

"Mike!"

"Hey, I was thinking, maybe you could come over tonight?"

"Tonight? But you're leaving tomorrow morning. Don't you have to pack?" I asked.

"I'm a guy, remember? I packed in like ten minutes."

"Ten minutes?" I snorted. "I'll bet you five bucks you forgot to pack something important."

"Like what?"

"Toothbrush, underwear..."

"Now that you mention it," he said, laughing, "I'd better go double-check."

"So, you really want me to come over?"

"Yup. My parents are going out to a charity dinner, but Mom said she'd help me make dinner for you."

"Whoa. Seriously? What are we having? Frozen corndogs?" I giggled.

"Now, now—no insulting my... I mean, my mom's cooking."

"Oh, all right. So what are you making?"

"How does gourmet macaroni and cheese with a salad sound? Or is that too pedestrian for your taste?"

I snorted. "Mac and cheese? Does it come in a blue box with the letters KRAFT on it?"

"No," he said indignantly. "This is gourmet macaroni and cheese. It's killer—one of my mom's best recipes."

I suddenly felt bad for making fun of him. "Actually, that sounds kind of good."

"You'll love it. Can you be over here by six o'clock?"

"Sure. I'll bring dessert," I answered.

"Perfect. See you at six."

I hung up and quickly walked over to our little book nook under the overhang of our kitchen countertop. I pulled out a cookbook and leafed through it until I found the dessert section.

"Yum. Brownies sound good."

***

An hour later, the smell of chocolate wafted through the air as I pulled the hot pan out of the oven.

Magically, Jackson appeared in the doorway, salivating like a pack animal.

"Don't even think about it."

"Why not?" he whined. "Brownies are my favorite."

"Well, these are for Mike and his family. I'm invited for dinner tonight."

"Oh, man. That's not fair."

I rolled my eyes. "Look, I'll make you another batch when I get home, all right?"

"Can't you just leave half of them here?" His lower lip jutted out.

"Nope. I'm taking the whole pan. I promise I'll make you a batch later."

He huffed and stomped heavily out of the kitchen.

Little brothers.

***

I arrived at Mike's right at six o'clock and walked up to the large wooden door, a pan of brownies in my hands.

Mike opened it before I could even knock.

"Hi, beautiful." He took the pan from me and kissed me. "Brownies, my favorite."

"You're lucky I made it here with the whole pan intact. I think Jackson may want to fight you for them."

He laughed. "I think I might win."

Kaya bounded up to me, her pink tongue lolling off to one side. She attacked my shoe laces and gave them a yank.

"Kaya!" Mike reprimanded. "You leave Jenny alone."

"Oh, it's okay." I knelt down to pet her, running my fingers through her soft fur. She looked up at me. I swear she was smiling. I plunked down on the floor, and she climbed into my lap. I cupped her snowy white face in my hands and kissed the top of her head. The silver-tipped fur along the ruff of her neck glittered like tinsel.

"She has really taken to you." Mike held out his hand to help me up off the floor.

"I love her too." I scooped the puppy off my lap and let Mike pull me up.

"C'mon, let's go see what's going on in the kitchen." He led me into the next room.

Mike's mom was just pulling a hot baking dish out of the oven. Steam escaped up into the kitchen, and the smell of cheesy goodness filled the air. She set the dish onto the black granite countertop and turned as Mike and I entered the kitchen.

"Hi, Mrs. Kramer," I said. "That smells delicious."

"Thanks. I hope you like it. Mike helped make the cheese sauce." She pulled the hot mitts off her hands and put them in a drawer. She was wearing a full-length sapphire gown and expensive-looking sandals. Her dark hair was swept into a formal up-do.

"Wow, that's a stunning dress." I cringed inwardly... was I being too much of a suck-up? But she really did look nice.

"Well, thank you." She beamed. "She's a good girl, Mike."

Mike put his arm around me. "Yeah, I know."

"All you have to do is make a salad," his mom told him. "I've left the recipe out for you, okay?"

He grinned. "I think I can handle the salad on my own. Thanks, Mom."

"Well, all right." She made her way out of the kitchen. "I'm going to put the finishing touches on my make-up. Mike, don't stay up too late, okay? We're leaving in the morning, and I don't want you to be impossible to wake up tomorrow."

"Yes, Mom, I know." He rolled his eyes.

"Jenny, it was a pleasure seeing you," Mrs. Kramer said.

"Same," I answered.

"Save me some of those brownies." She smiled and then whisked out of the room, her perfume drifting in her wake.

I waited until I heard her shoes tip-tap up the solid wood staircase. "Aren't your parents worried about leaving us here alone?" I asked.

Mike grinned as he opened the fridge and took out some lettuce. "Not really. They trust me… and I promised them I wouldn't attack you or anything."

I laughed. "Hopefully you had your fingers crossed behind your back when you promised."

Mike's eyebrows shot upward in surprise. "Really?"

Oh my God. Why were these strange words coming out of my mouth? "I was just kidding."

Mike's green eyes glinted mischievously. "Well, I hope not. I kind of like that idea. But I did promise my parents…."

I wondered if he was just messing with me. I had no idea what went on in the minds of eighteen-year-old boys. I guessed that most of their thoughts weren't G-rated.

Mike got out an assortment of ingredients. "Feel up to making the dressing?"

He pushed the recipe toward me.

"Sure." I went to the sink to wash my hands.

"I'll chop the veggies." He got more produce out of the refrigerator and retrieved a cutting board from a drawer near the sink.

"See you in a few hours!" Mike's dad called from the foyer.

"Have a nice dinner," his mom said. The door clicked behind them.

Mike smiled, his eyes twinkling. "I thought they'd never leave."

He pulled me into his arms and kissed me. I giggled and put a dab of the freshly made salad dressing on his nose.

"Hey," he said, and smeared some on my cheek.

"Truce!" I called as I wiped the drip off my face.

"Well, all right," he said, feigning disappointment. "Let's get the food dished up. Do you want to eat outside? It's a nice night."

"Sure." I scooped the food onto the plates.

Mike poured some lemonade from the pitcher on the counter into two fancy wine goblets and carried them outside onto the deck. I grabbed the plates while he came back for the utensils.

After everything was out on the table, we settled down to eat. I ignored the salad and went straight for the pasta. One bite of the heavenly cheese, and I was a goner.

I savored the richness. "This is really, really good."

Mike nodded as he chewed. "I know. This is a recipe that will have to stay in the family forever. I think I could it eat it at least once a week."

As I ate, my vision began to blur. Oh, no. A vision was coming on. I tried to fight it, but it came anyway. Mike melted away as a man's form began to take shape in front of me.

Flash.

Suddenly, I was a little boy, sitting in a stark white kitchen—staring down at my plastic bowl, the artificial fluorescent orange noodles congealed in a puddle around the edges.

"Why aren't you eating, Devon? Macaroni and cheese was always your favorite!"

I shook my head slowly as I stuck my fork upright into the stuff in the bowl.

"Where's Mommy? I want my mom."

"Sorry, buddy, your mom doesn't want you anymore," the man said sadly.

"You're lying!" My face burned with anger. "Mommy loves me! She says that every day!"

"No, Devon. I'm sorry. She doesn't love you. She lied to you."

"No!" I dumped the macaroni and cheese onto the table. "You're the liar!"

The man's face reddened, and he stood to his full height, towering over me. I shrank back, shaking.

34

"Your mother obviously didn't teach you to respect your elders. Guess it's up to me to teach you," he said and yanked me off my chair.

Thunk!

"Jenny!" Mike jumped to his feet and picked me up off the deck. "Are you okay?"

I blinked and shook my head. "I don't know."

"What happened?" He helped me sit back down in the chair.

"It was a vision." I explained the other visions of the boy being abducted in the park. Mike leaned forward as I talked, his face pale.

"Oh my God!" He got up out of his chair. "Did you call the police? They've got to find this kid!"

"I've been working with Detective Coalfield. He thinks the man might be related to Devon."

"Like—his dad?"

"I don't think so. Vince McLeod was out of town when the boy was taken."

"Is there anything else you can do to help find him?" He ran his fingers through his hair.

"I don't know. I feel really useless." I pushed my plate away. "I mean, I know I'm getting this information so I can help him, but it's not enough. It's really frustrating."

"I can imagine." Mike sat down again. "Do you think there might be a way to make the information come more quickly? Or get more each time you have a vision?"

"Possibly. I'll ask Celine in class next week."

"Class?"

I explained about taking Celine's summer intensive workshop.

"That sounds like it will be really helpful. Maybe she can give you some more tips on how to find Devon."

"God, I hope so."

35

***

We cleared our half-eaten dinner off the outdoor table and carried everything back to the kitchen.

I tried brushing thoughts of Devon out of my mind for the moment. It was torture, thinking about him and what he must be going through. I wished with every ounce of me that I could help him. Unfortunately, the information was just not coming.

But at the same time, I was with Mike, and it was our last night together for at least a week. We would have just one day more together when he returned from his trip and I left for mine. To push the thoughts of Devon away, I changed the subject to school.

"Have you decided on a major yet?" I asked as we scraped and rinsed our plates in the sink.

"Of course." He began loading the dishwasher. "The University of Washington has a pretty good theatre department. I'm going to go for a BA in Drama."

"That's great. Are your parents fine with that? I'm not sure my parents would approve if I chose drama as a major."

"Why not?" He put the last of the extra food in the fridge. "My parents seem to be okay with it."

I shrugged. "Dad thinks I should go for something practical—like dental hygiene or nursing. That's just not me."

Mike laughed, and tugged me out into the living room. "Dental hygiene? You?"

"I know. Somehow, telling a girl who loves to be on stage that they should pick plaque off of some guy's teeth... well, it's just not right."

He grinned and led me deeper into the room. For some reason, I had never been in here before. We had usually hung out in either the kitchen or the family room. A massive floor-to-ceiling river rock fireplace took my breath away. I turned around, taking it all in. I looked up at the vaulted ceilings and big wooden beams.

"Wow." I tilted my head back. "How do you guys change the light bulbs up there?"

"With a very tall ladder." He nudged me over to an expansive leather couch.

I shivered, wrapped my arms around myself, and sat down.

"Cold?" He pulled the French doors leading to the other side of the deck closed. "This side of the house doesn't seem to warm up, even in the summer. Guess it's because of all the trees."

Mike flipped a switch on the wall and the enormous gas fireplace was instantly ablaze, filling the room with a soft, warm glow.

He sat down beside me and wrapped his arm around my shoulders.

"So." He turned toward me. "If you don't want to be a dental hygienist, what do you want to be?"

"I'm not sure. At least I have one more year of high school to figure it out."

"You've got plenty of time to decide." Mike cradled my face in his hands. "We've got plenty of time to be together too."

My insides melted. Thoughts of school, dental hygiene, and Devon drifted away as he kissed me tenderly. All I cared about was Mike. I could easily let the rest of the world fall away—as long as he was in my life, nothing else mattered.

He brushed the hair from my forehead and whispered, "I wish my parents weren't coming home tonight."

The thought of me spending the night here with him thrilled and scared me. Was I ready for this? This was possibly the most important relationship I would ever have with another human being. As scared as I was, it felt right somehow.

37

I kissed him back with a passion I never knew I had. He seemed surprised, but then let go and was drawn into the moment.

A loud crackle from the fireplace startled me. I opened my eyes and turned my head to watch as the flames flared up and burned more intensely.

Flash.

The fire danced over the surface of the water. I could hear shrill screaming coming from the burning boat. I heard the sounds, but I was already pulling away from my body. I watched it as my soul hovered over the water; watched my body spiraling downward into the murky depths of the ocean.

My eyes flew open.

"What?" Mike pulled me closer. "Let's not lose the moment."

I pushed him away, all thoughts of romance dissipating in an instant.

I sighed.

My gift was seriously damaging my love life.

Chapter 7

"Protection," Celine announced.

"What?" asked one of the students. We were all sitting on the wood floor of the Intuitive Institute. The building was an industrial-style loft near Pike Place Market—a combination of wood, steel, and lots of windows up high to let in the light.

Celine's musical laughter drifted up into the ceiling above.

"Protection is what we will be learning about today. It is the single most important lesson any psychic should learn."

"Uh—I don't get it," a skinny teenage boy with dark hair said as he looked at Celine.

I glanced over at him. He seemed really familiar to me. Where had I seen him before?

"Well, Benny," Celine said, and turned to address him. "When you are an intuitive, you are open to so much sensory input coming at you from so many places, it can be completely overwhelming."

Celine began turning as she talked so all of us could see her face. "How many of you have seen anything *disturbing?*" she asked. "As in, a disturbing vision."

Every person sitting in the circle slowly raised their hands, sneaking peeks at each other to make sure they weren't the only ones.

Celine continued. "And how many of you have been terrified by things that you've seen?"

Again, we all raised our hands.

"How many of you find it difficult to be in a public place with lots of people?"

I thought of going to places like the mall or even school; the thoughts and happenings of people—the turmoil in their lives... all of those emotions coming at me from every which way.

I raised my hand. I looked around the circle and noticed that most hands were up in answer to this one too.

"Okay. So, protection," she said, "is there to keep you from going getting hurt by all of this stuff coming at you. It's putting your shields up to deflect the thoughts, worries, and fears that are running rampant all around you."

"Protection from other people's baggage then?" asked a woman who was about my mom's age.

"Yes, and also from darker spirits," she added. "They can be really scary if you aren't prepared for them."

Darker spirits? Oh great. Now I had to worry about bad guys *and* dark spirits. So far, I hadn't run into any of those. I hoped I never would.

"First, I want you to sit cross-legged."

Everyone shifted around the floor a bit, adjusting their positions.

"Now, close your eyes. Imagine a white light around your entire body—like a pure white aura encircling you."

She was quiet for a moment, giving us a chance to picture the white light.

"Now repeat after me. Let the white light of the Holy Spirit surround and protect me."

"Let the white light of the Holy Spirit surround and protect me," we murmured in unison.

"Spirit, only show me things that I need to see to help myself or the people who ask me for help."

We repeated the mantra together.

"That's the most basic prayer we can do for protection. The more you learn and develop your skills, the longer the prayers can get. There may be a time when the danger is pretty great and you'll need powerful prayers to combat the dark energy around you."

I swallowed hard. I was getting a little freaked out by the words "danger" and "dark energy." I wasn't really keen on repeating the events of a few months ago.

Celine turned and looked at me. "Jenny, are you okay with this so far?"

My face reddened, the heat traveling from my chin to my forehead.

At the mention of my name, the boy named Benny glanced at me. I could tell that he recognized me... and then I realized where I had seen him before. He was a student at Newport High School.

"Jenny?" Celine asked again. "Are you okay?"

"Uh, yeah," I replied, my face still burning red. "It's just a little scary, that's all. I mean, thinking about the dark stuff."

"That's okay," she said. "But at least you're now learning how to deal with the things you see, even if they are frightening. The techniques that you're learning for protection will give you the power to shield yourself. And they'll provide you with a measure of comfort as well."

The students were all silent for a few moments, letting the information soak in. I couldn't stop thinking about this Benny kid, though. I just hoped that he wouldn't go back to school and tell everyone that I was in this psychic class. Although, I was pretty sure that in doing so, he would blow his cover too. Not that he had anything to lose. He wasn't very popular. In fact, he was bullied on a regular basis. I just hoped he was able to keep a juicy secret instead of blabbing it to everyone.

"So, next," Celine interrupted my thoughts, "let's learn a hymn. This is something that I've put together over the years. It really helps to calm and center me."

Some of the students shifted uncomfortably.

"Oh, it's okay!" Celine laughed. "None of us will be judging your singing. And we'll all sing together, so even if you're not musical, you won't stand out."

Nervous laughter echoed through the large room.

Celine sat down in the middle of the circle. "Everyone reach out and hold hands."

I linked hands with the two people on either side of me. Their thoughts bombarded me.

"This is weird."

"What should I make for dinner?"

"Maybe I shouldn't have signed up for this class."

"Oh shoot! I forgot to take the chicken out of the freezer!"

I yanked my hands away. "What the?" I muttered.

Celine turned to face me. I looked up, and there were other people having the same sort of reaction as me. Several others had dropped the hands of the people next to them.

She smiled. "Ah yes, that's normal."

I should have known that would happen.

"Let's begin again by closing our eyes and repeating our protection mantra," she said.

Together we said, "Let the white light of the Holy Spirit surround and protect me."

"And now," Celine continued, "Spirit, only show me things that I need to help myself or the people who ask me for help."

We repeated it. Already, I could feel a calm wash over me and I began breathing more deeply.

"Let's link hands once again."

The thoughts of the students on either side of me were still there, but muted. I could focus on Celine's voice much better.

Celine began to sing and then stopped at the end of each stanza so we could sing it back. I had no idea what the words meant. They seemed to be in another language. The effect, though, was amazing. The calm spread throughout my body. I felt peaceful, and the sense of belonging was so strong, I didn't want it to end.

We sang the hymn over and over again until we knew it by heart.

At the end of the last verse, Celine was quiet, the stillness settling in around our shoulders and seeping into our bodies.

"How did that feel?" she asked.

"Great," I answered as many others agreed.

"I use that before I do readings for my clients, or whenever I have to find the answer to something that I really need to know."

Questions about Devon popped into my head. I slowly raised my hand in the air.

"Yes?" Celine turned to me.

"If there is something that we want to know, is there anything we can do to make the information come faster? Like if it's urgent?"

"Well, it depends," she answered, searching my face. "Sometimes you can find answers more quickly if you meditate regularly. And sometimes you'll get a rush of information just doing daily things like taking a shower or something like that."

A chuckle rang out in the silence of the room. We all turned to an older man who looked amused.

"Frank, do you have an anecdote to share? Or a comment?" Celine asked.

"Not really," he said. "The shower thing just kind of struck me as funny. I mean, I'll probably never take a shower without thinking that some spirit is watching me come up with a question... naked."

Celine grinned. "It does sound a little silly, I'll grant you that. But actually, if you ever get stuck on something or you just aren't getting an answer you need, play in the water. Water is a great channeler of energy."

I thought about running home to take an extra shower right after the class. Or maybe a walk on the beach would help me find Devon.

"We're going to do one more exercise today before I let you go," Celine said. "Since we've already said our prayer and asked for protection, let's just get to the next step. First, I want you to think of a question. Take a minute to really think about what you want to know and then speak it within yourself."

My mind raced, churning through the dozens of questions I could ask. First and foremost, I thought about Devon. Questions about my future with Mike danced through my brain as well. But those were selfish. The little boy was more important than my teenage romance. I finally settled on "Who took Devon McLeod?"

"This may not work for you every single time. So, if you don't get anything right now, try not to be disappointed."

The older man who had chuckled about the shower cleared his throat.

"Yes, Frank?"

"How do we know if the answer we get is the true answer?" he asked.

"For some people, the answer comes from their heart, some people hear their own voice, and others hear someone else's voice. Some even hear the voice of an ancestor. Others might see a vision. It's different for everyone. But it should ring true to you. You should feel its truth in your heart. Does everyone have their question?"

Celine asked, sitting down in the middle of the circle and crossing her legs in a meditation pose.

Murmurs of assent rippled through the room.

"Good." She placed her hands on each of her knees. "Close your eyes. Now, we are going to create our Sacred Container. We have our own little protective bubble here to keep us safe."

I opened one eye and peeked around the room as people shifted a little uncomfortably, wondering what would happen next.

"Dear God, Spirit Guides, Angels, and all the beautiful spirits who are here to help us, please come into our circle. We invite you in. We ask that you help us serve the highest good and bless us with grace." She paused a moment. "Think of your question and speak it in your mind."

I thought, *"Who took Devon McLeod?"*

"If we have the question," Celine went on, "then we have the answer. Be still and listen."

Again, I thought, *"Who took Devon McLeod?"*

We sat in silence. The muffled sounds of the city slowly faded into the background.

Silence.

Breathing.

Then a garbled whisper in my ear, *"Hsssdddd."*

I sucked in my breath. The whisper came again—so real that it felt as if someone was leaning over my shoulder and saying it directly into my ear. *"His Dad took him."*

My eyes popped open. I was just about to get up and run from the room to make a call when I noticed what was going on within the circle. There were people in there.

Spirits hovered a few inches above the floor. Semi-transparent spirits. They were talking and miming things to the participants of the circle. And though the students had their eyes closed, some of them smiled and listened intently.

I rubbed my eyes and looked again. Still there. I watched in complete awe for a few minutes. Slowly, the ghost people faded and disappeared. Some of the students were opening their eyes and looking around. When the last spirit vanished, I got up and approached Celine.

I crouched down to where she was sitting and quietly said, "I need to go make a phone call."

She studied my face for a few moments and seemed to understand that it was important. "Go ahead."

I stood up and quickly slipped out the door into the back hallway that led to the bathroom. I tugged my phone out of my pocket and dialed.

"Detective Coalfield," the deep voice on the other end of the line answered.

"Hi, it's Jenny," I said breathlessly.

"Jenny! What's up?"

"I just got some information on the little boy, Devon McLeod. It was his dad. I know you said that Vince McLeod was out of town, but he must have fooled you guys or something."

"Whoa, wait," he said. "His dad had a really solid alibi. We talked to his boss; he was at work."

"Couldn't he have left work long enough to take Devon?" I asked.

"Jenny, his dad works in a fish processing plant up in Alaska. He couldn't just leave town and kidnap his son in Renton."

I bit my lip. "Well, I just *know* it was his dad. Can you prove he was at work for sure?"

"The processing plant has a time card punch. Employees walk in and punch their time card. That's how the employer knows if they worked all the hours they were supposed to—and if they showed up late or something like that," he answered.

"Do they know when the employees leave? Could he have left early?" I asked, searching my brain for any kind of explanation.

"They should know. The employee has to punch out when they are done with their shift. We have records showing he worked a full shift on the day Devon disappeared."

I blew out a breath. "There has to be *some* explanation."

"Well, I'll give Vince McLeod a call and ask him a few more questions," he offered.

"Did he leave Alaska to come look for Devon? Is he here?" I asked.

"No, he said he had to work," the detective said.

"What? You're kidding me!" I was stunned. "His own father wouldn't take some time off to find his missing son? If that had been me, my dad would have dropped everything and jumped on the next plane!"

"I know, I thought it was odd too," Detective Coalfield answered. "But the guy explained that this was the first job he has been able to hold onto. He thought he would be fired if he left."

"Still, that's not the kind of thing a normal dad would do."

"I agree," he admitted. "But you'd be surprised how many people make unusual decisions. If I've learned anything about people in this line of work, it's that not everybody makes the same choices that I would make."

I thought about that for a moment and realized how true that was.

"Anyway," Detective Coalfield continued, "I'm going to give Devon's dad a call and question him a bit more. I'll contact his co-workers as well to see if they remember him being at work the whole day. It could be someone else punched his card or something."

"That's true," I said. "Someone else could have covered for him."

"It's worth another look, that's for sure," he added.

I felt so much better knowing that he was going to delve deeper into Vince McLeod's alibi.

"Thanks, Detective," I said. "If I get any more information, I'll call you right away."

"No, thank *you*, Jenny," he answered. "It's great to have leads like this. Otherwise, it's like trying to find a needle in a haystack."

I snuck quietly back into class and sat down in the empty spot in the circle.

"So, what do you think?" Celine asked us. "Did you get the answers you were hoping for? Does anyone want to share their experience?"

A middle-aged woman sitting next to me slowly raised her hand, looking nervous.

"Yes, Judy, go ahead," Celine said.

"Well, my question was about my daughter. I wanted to know if she would be able to turn her life around." She swallowed hard and then continued. "She's got a drug problem."

Celine nodded. "And? Did you get an answer?"

"I think so." She bit her lip. "I think I heard, 'In a few years,' or something like that."

"Did you get any visual images with the information?" Celine asked.

The woman furrowed her brow as she closed her eyes. "Yes, but it doesn't make any sense to me."

Celine waited while Judy gathered her thoughts.

"I saw a big mountain, covered in snow. Then, I saw a beautiful brown owl flying across the sky." She opened her eyes and continued. "The owl soared over the mountain and then disappeared into the sunset. What could that mean?"

Celine smiled, looking very pleased. "Yes, yes, that's very good! The mountain symbolizes an obstacle—something your daughter is going to have to get over. The owl represents wisdom."

Judy still looked confused.

Before she could ask another question, Celine went on. "So, you see, the owl flew over the mountain, clearing her obstacle. By doing so, she has gained the wisdom she needs to move on."

"Ohhhh." Judy's voice broke, tears running down her cheeks. "Oh, that is just the best news I've heard in a long time."

I felt relieved for her.

"Anyone else?" Celine asked, pointing to another person with their hand up.

***

After Celine dismissed us, I left the loft and walked back on Western Avenue toward Pike Place Market. I wanted to pick up some salmon and fresh vegetables to make dinner for my family. I didn't do that very often, and I knew my mom would love it.

As I made my way to the market, I heard a soft shuffling behind me. I casually glanced over my right shoulder and caught a glimpse of Benny, the kid from class. He smiled uncertainly at me.

"Hi!" I let him catch up to me. "Weird seeing someone from school at a psychic summer camp, huh?"

He looked a little taken aback and then laughed. "I guess."

"You're not going to tell anybody about this, are you?" I asked.

He shook his head. "Who would I tell? My one friend in the world is on vacation in Maine."

"Oh," I said, embarrassed that I had even brought it up.

An awkward silence passed between the two of us.

"So, what do you think of Celine?" I asked, trying to break the ice a little.

"She's interesting." He shoved his hands in his pockets.

We walked by a French bakery. The smell of freshly baked croissants and coffee drifted through the warm summer air.

I turned to Benny and lightly laid my hand on his arm. "Hey, do you want to grab a cup of coffee and something yummy from in there?" I tipped my chin in the direction of the bakery.

"What?" he said. "You want to have coffee with me?"

I stopped and searched his eyes for sarcasm. But he wasn't kidding. He seemed truly astounded that I had asked him to sit and talk.

"Of course!" I gently guided him to the café. "I'm buying. Iced lattes and croissants all right with you? Or would you rather have something else?"

"That's fine with me."

I took a twenty-dollar bill from my purse and paid.

He just stood there, his mouth hanging open a little.

"I'll wait for our stuff. Why don't you grab a table?"

Still looking like he was in shock, he slowly moved around the small seating area. Just then, a couple got up and left a table near the window. Benny reached the table and sat down stiffly.

Was I that unapproachable? He seemed like he was scared to talk to me, or even look at me for that matter. As my senior year was coming up, I made a mental note to myself to talk to more people outside my little social bubble. I wondered what Benny thought of me. Did he think I was a mean girl?

"Two iced lattes and two croissants." The barista pushed the order toward me.

"Thanks." I tucked the croissant bags under my arm and carefully carried the coffees to our table.

I set everything down and took a seat opposite Benny. Taking a big sip of my coffee through my straw, I watched him as he nervously drew designs in the condensation on the side of his cup.

"Benny?"

His head snapped up, and then he looked down again almost immediately.

"Is there something wrong?" I asked.

"No," he mumbled. "Well, kind of."

"What is it?" I unearthed the croissant from its brown bag and ripped off a corner.

He looked at me hesitantly. "You know how you were worried that I would tell someone about you attending this class?"

"Yes." I delicately popped a small piece of croissant into my mouth.

"I guess I'm kind of worried that you'll tell people at school that you saw *me* in the class." He immediately looked down at his hands again.

I almost choked on my croissant. "Seriously? Why would I do that?"

He quickly took a sip of his latte. "Because it's gossip. Being the person who gets to spill a really juicy secret and then laughing about it with your friends is fun for some people, right?"

Now it was my turn to have my mouth hang open. "You really think that's what I'm all about?"

"Well, I don't know, but you're a cheerleader, and everybody likes you."

"Okay, correction: I *was* a cheerleader. I haven't been a cheerleader since I recovered from my concussion. And even when I was a cheerleader, I didn't do stuff like that."

His face began to turn an alarming shade of red. "Oh, I really screwed up, didn't I? I'm sorry."

"Look, it's okay." My heart rate began to return to normal. "You're right. There are a lot of kids who would have done exactly what you described. But even though I don't look it on the outside, on the inside, I've always *felt* different. I kept waiting, you know. For someone to figure out that I'm a freak. I thought for sure that somebody would discover my secret and this nice 'normal' life would be over."

He looked shocked again.

I laughed, trying to ease the tension. "It's okay. Some of my friends *did* find out this year, and it wasn't nearly as bad as I had imagined it."

He smiled a little and began eating his croissant. "At least you don't have two strikes against you."

"Two?"

"Yeah, I have two," he answered. "I'm psychic *and* I'm gay."

"Oh," I said. I took another sip of my latte, rattling the ice cubes around in my cup. The truth was, I knew he was gay. That was part of the reason he got bullied in school so much. "Well, I don't care if you're psychic or gay. So what?"

"So what?" he echoed. "So, if you only knew what my life was like…"

"I didn't mean it that way," I said, meeting his eyes. They were blue, like my own. "I meant, so what if you're gay? There isn't anything wrong with that."

He raised his eyebrows. "Not everybody thinks that way, though."

"I know, but even the kids who pick on you probably don't care if you're gay or not. They just want to make someone else feel bad so that they'll feel better about themselves. Twenty years from now, they will probably be living in their parents' basement, playing video games and wishing they were you."

He laughed. "Okay, then what will I be doing?"

"You'll be a TV star, a lawyer, a doctor. I don't know." I laughed. "What do you want to be?"

"Anyone but me," he answered almost too quickly.

I winced. "God, Benny. That's so sad. We have to do something about that."

"Oh, yeah, like what?"

"Well, for one thing, you can start hanging out with me. Maybe we can turn you into 'the cool gay kid' at school."

His eyes looked like they would pop out of his head, and then he burst into a spontaneous fit of laughter. The other customers turned around to stare at us.

"Shhhhh," I whispered, grinning. "This is not the image you want to portray. You gotta be cool."

He snorted and swallowed his laughter. "If you can do that, then you're a miracle worker."

"I might just be." If I could help Benny transition into a cool guy, then maybe anything was possible. I could help find Devon McLeod. And if I could help find Devon McLeod, maybe I could figure out what my other dream was all about. A burning boat, a lost boy, and the transformation of one of the least popular kids at school— this was going to be an interesting summer.

Chapter 8

The next day, Benny and I sat side-by-side in the circle on the floor. Now that everyone had gotten to know one another a little, people were visiting, talking and laughing quietly together.

"I wonder what Celine is going to have us do today?" I whispered to Benny.

He shrugged. "I hope it doesn't involve Ouija boards. Those things creep me out."

"Me too. But she doesn't strike me as a Ouija board person."

Just then, Celine came in carrying a basket of magazines. She dumped them out in the middle of the circle. She walked to the back of the room and opened the doors to a tall steel cabinet lined with shelves, and pulled out another basket. She spilled out the contents next to the magazines—glue sticks and scissors.

"Can everyone go pick a poster board from the counter?" She gestured to the long table next to the cabinet. Looking very artsy today, she was wearing faded blue jeans, a white cotton blouse, and a hemp macramé vest.

Everyone got up and shuffled to the back of the room. There was a stack of poster boards in various colors fanned out on the marbled surface of the counter. I chose a bright lime green poster board and sat back down in my place in the circle.

When everyone had picked out the color they wanted and were sitting in their spots, Celine cleared her throat.

"We are going to make collages," she announced.

"What?" Frank huffed. "I didn't sign up for an art class."

A couple of people cracked up and nodded in agreement.

"Well, yesterday I wasn't judging you on your singing ability." Celine smiled. "Today, I'm not judging you on your artistic ability."

"That's a relief," he grumbled.

"This is not an art lesson," Celine continued as she walked the perimeter of our circle. "It's a lesson in symbols."

Most of the class looked confused, including me.

"Trust me, I'll explain later. For now, I want you to look through these magazines, and see what you are attracted to. Cut out the pictures that you are drawn to; those that mean something to you."

"And then what?" asked another student.

Celine smiled. "You'll see. I promise. There is a point to this."

We all settled in, paging through magazines and choosing images to cut out and glue onto our poster boards. Once I got started, I was really into it. At first, I found pictures of beautiful flowers, sunshine, and sunny beaches. But then, I found photos of a raven, an artist's rendering of a Civil War battlefield, lightning, and a purple sky darkening into evening. I worked feverishly, shutting out everyone around me. I didn't even notice what Benny was doing.

"All right then," Celine said, interrupting my flow. "Let's stop at this point. I want everyone to take their poster board to the back and prop it up against the wall."

She demonstrated by taking Frank's poster board and carrying it to the long countertop at the back of the room, leaning it against the wall.

We obediently followed suit. Once everyone's work was on display, we stepped back. The boards were vastly different. There were some definite themes going on. Frank's art was plastered in military-themed images— naval ships, bombers, Army recruitment posters. There were also smaller photos of families, women with children, and a small pink heart which seemed out of character with the rest of the images.

"Let's talk about Frank's art," Celine said pointing to the first board. "Would anyone like to take a guess as to why he chose these images?"

"What do you mean?" asked a young woman next to me. "Do you want us to guess why he chose these images, or what his life is like, or what?"

"I want you to look at the board and give me your impressions. It could be about his life or a life he would like, or anything that comes to mind when you look at the pictures. Would you like to give it a try, Sandra?"

The young woman hesitated. "Uh, okay. My guess is that Frank was a military guy. With all the photos of ships and stuff, I think he must have been a career military man."

Frank grunted his affirmation.

"What else?" Celine asked.

"Looks like he has a family."

We all turned to Frank to see if he would agree. He pursed his lips, and his shoulders tightened as his hands clenched into fists at his sides.

"Is that correct, Frank?" Celine asked.

"Yeah, sort of," he muttered.

We all stared at him, waiting for an explanation.

"I did have a family." He ran his fingers through his gray buzz-cut. "I just didn't make time for them. My country was always my top priority."

"What happened to them?" Benny asked quietly.

"My wife was left alone with our three kids a lot. She got really lonely, I guess."

He cleared his throat and was silent for a moment. "One day, I came home early after an important mission. I could hear the kids playing in the backyard. When I first entered our home, I didn't see her. So, I went down the hall—the door to the bedroom was closed."

I could guess what was coming next and I swallowed hard, thinking how Frank must have felt.

"I opened the bedroom door, figuring she was taking a nap." He stopped again and took a deep breath. "But she wasn't taking a nap."

We exchanged uneasy glances, waiting for Frank to continue.

"She was in bed with my best friend."

The room was silent. No one even dared to take a breath.

"Oh my God," Sandra whispered.

"Yeah," Frank said.

"What did you do?" I asked.

"I yelled, raged, and beat the crap out of my so-called friend," he answered. "My wife screamed and tried to pull us apart. I pushed her back down on the bed. I was so angry. I'd never felt so betrayed in my life."

Frank seemed to deflate right in front of us, his tall strong stature shrunken and meek.

"Then I left. Never even said goodbye to my kids. I just left, and I never turned back. I had a buddy pack up all my stuff for me. But I never saw her or my children again."

"You mean, you still haven't talked to them?" someone asked.

"I know it sounds terrible. I was a bad father, it's true," he said sadly. "I was just so hurt—I couldn't face them. I couldn't think of them. I had to leave it all behind."

Sandra was clearly taken aback. "But, how could you not talk to your children?" she sputtered. "It wasn't *their* fault!"

"You're absolutely right," Frank said quietly. "And that is pretty much why I find myself here, in this class. I need to get in touch with my human side. I spent so many years focusing on my career. I want to search for the family I left behind. But before I do that, I need to fix things inside of me. I need to heal my old wounds and make things right."

We were silent for a moment, taking in Frank's story.

"It's very brave of you to share that with us, Frank," Celine said quietly. "Thank you. Let's move on to the next poster."

She pointed to the collage next to Frank. "Benny? Is this yours?"

"Yes," he mumbled, casting his eyes down to the painted concrete floor.

I was astounded at the emotional impact of his work. My eyes traveled from the bottom of the piece to the top, noting how very different the two hemispheres were. All of the images on the bottom were in gray tones; cold stone cathedrals, a prison, steel-colored clouds, a dark hued raincoat, an angry set of masks, and a dark forest. As my eyes drifted upward along the board, my heart began to lift. Color slowly emerged from the bottom to the top: a circle of children wearing brightly colored clothes holding hands, a dandelion gone to seed—a single white tuft floating away into the blue sky, smiling faces, carnival-colored hot air balloons drifting ever higher into the atmosphere, and two people holding hands.

"It's beautiful, Benny." Celine said. "Would you like to explain it?"

Benny pointed to the bottom. "Where I began."

He gestured to the top of the board and said simply, "Where I'd like to go."

I swallowed hard.

Flash.

"Not good enough."

"Why can't you be more like your brother?"

"Art lessons? I don't think so. I signed you up for basketball camp."

"Why don't you invite a girl to the dance?"

"I wish you were never born."

I was standing with my knees wobbling, my body shaking. I shook off the images and steadied myself. Looking around the room, I noticed that tears were rolling down the cheeks of several of the students—they clearly felt Benny's sadness. Had they seen what I had seen? Tears escaped the inside corner of my eyes and slowly traveled down the length of my face, dripping onto my shoulder. I reached out and gripped Benny's hand and squeezed it tightly.

"I'm so sorry," I whispered.

One by one, the students stepped in closer to Benny, wrapping their arms around him until we were one entwined huddle with him in the center.

When we finally stepped back, Celine said, "I'm very proud of all of you. That was truly beautiful."

We wiped away our tears.

"Shall we move on? Jenny, is this one yours?" she asked.

I nodded. I had no idea what my images meant—I simply chose them because I was drawn to them. Wondering what Celine would say, I scanned her face. Her eyes widened as she studied the images.

Celine's voice shook. "The raven... a harbinger of death or a bad omen, the purple night sky... purple is associated with powerful visions, the civil war battlefield is associated with an upcoming fight, even the flowers you've chosen."

My body felt like lead. What was she talking about? "Flowers? I chose them because they were beautiful—how could they be bad?"

"They aren't bad necessarily," Celine said softly. "But different flowers symbolize different things. The flowers you've chosen... oleander means caution, poppy represents eternal sleep, the black rose symbolizes death. Do you see where I'm going with this?"

I took a deep breath. "No. I don't know."

"Jenny," she said breathlessly, "you are in grave danger."

Chapter 9

After class, I fought my way through afternoon traffic. Bumper-to-bumper congestion gave me time to let what happened settle in my brain. I was in danger. That much was clear. Now what? Did I ignore the symbols? Was Celine full of crap? The other students' collages seemed very accurate and pertinent to their lives. I really had no reason to believe she was wrong. I wondered if this related to the visions I was having. I hadn't used any images of boats or fires in my collage. It was all very confusing.

By the time I finally made it home, I had decided that I couldn't worry about it too much. But if someone handed me a black rose, I wasn't going to stick around to find out if they were going to off me or not.

I opened the door to my house and was nearly pounced on by my dad.

"Dad, what are you doing home so early?" I said.

"Jim's got the boat all ready to go!" He hugged me. "Oh, and it's a beauty too. You are going to love it."

Jesus, he was acting like a big puppy.

"Oh, okay." I pulled away from his bear hug.

"It's moored in Elliot Bay. You want to go check it out with me?"

How could I say no to that puppy enthusiasm? "Okay, do you want to go now?"

"Yeah." His blue eyes twinkled.

"Mind if I freshen up and then call Mike really quick before we go?" I asked.

"Sure, but don't talk on the phone too long. I'm anxious to give you the grand tour."

"What about Mom and Jackson? Don't you want to wait for them?"

"Actually, they are meeting us over there. Mom is picking Jackson up from soccer camp, and they're heading over soon."

I ran up the stairs, and then slipped into my room. I dug my phone out of my bag and called Mike.

"Hello?" his voice crackled. "Jenny?"

"Yes, it's me!"

"It's good to hear your voice," he said.

"Ditto. How is your trip?"

"It's good. I miss you, though. We have a lot to talk about when I get back," he said.

I sat down on my bed. "We won't have a lot of time, since I'm leaving on my trip on Monday. That only leaves us a day to be together."

"I know, but we'll have time to talk." His voice distorted into a broken blurb.

"Talk?"

"Hey Jenny, the connection is breaking up. We're heading into a cove and I'm sure I'll lose signal. See you soon, okay?"

"Uh, okay." Before I could say anything else, the call ended.

I set my phone down on my desk and stared at it. What did he mean, we'll have time to talk?

"Jenny," Dad yelled from the bottom of the stairs. "Ready to go?"

"Be right there!" My two second conversation with Mike left me feeling unsettled.

***

"Isn't she gorgeous?" Dad said proudly as we walked down the length of the dock.

Mom, Jackson, and I looked at each other.

"Uh, which one is 'she?'" Mom asked.

Dad laughed. "That one!"

He gestured to the boat in the last slip to the left. Despite my reluctance to go on the trip, I had to admit it was pretty cool. It was a fishing boat—white with teak decks and handrails. It looked large enough to accommodate the four of us, plus Callie's dad. I suppose we would feel like sardines after being forced into semi-tight quarters after a while, but it was only for about two weeks.

"That's the boat?" Jackson asked.

"Uh huh." My dad grinned. "What do you think?"

Jackson shrugged. "I thought it would be bigger."

"What are you talking about? It's amazing. That's a thirty-six foot Grand Banks Classic you're looking at. What more could you want?" He slugged Jackson playfully on the arm.

"A yacht," my brother said with a yawn and a stretch. "Or maybe a cruise ship. With an all-you-can-eat buffet."

I rolled my eyes. "Twerp."

Jackson stuck his tongue out at me. I gave him a sour face in return.

"Actually, I think it's really awesome," I said.

Dad clapped me on the back. "Come on board, everyone!"

He went first and held out his hand to me. I balanced on the edge of the dock before stepping onto the narrow ladder up to the deck. Jackson and Mom were right behind me. Once onboard, we stood wondering what to check out first. My brother darted off to the bow, and I decided to go check out the inside and the sleeping arrangements. I

63

walked down the narrow side deck and slipped into the door of the main cabin.

"Wait until you see the engine, Mary." I could hear Dad droning on about the horsepower.

I said a silent prayer for my mom that she wouldn't die of sheer boredom listening to boat babble and surveyed the room. The inside of the cabin was detailed in a light teak finish. There was an eating or sitting area with white cushions in an L-shape, complete with a dining table with leaves that folded up and down. The galley was nicer than I had imagined, with a small oven and stovetop, a microwave, and a refrigerator. A short set of stairs led me to two bedrooms, one with a full-sized bed and one with a twin-sized bed.

Where were Jackson and I going to sleep? The larger bedroom would obviously be for my mom and dad, and I assumed that Callie's dad would be sleeping in the room with the twin-sized bed. I certainly hoped they weren't going to make us sleep up on deck. I imagined myself rolling off it in the middle of the night, making a gentle splash as I hit the frigid water. I shivered.

In the bow area, I found two beds meeting where the V-shape merged. Ugh. I would have to share this space with Jackson. At least I didn't have to lie next to him.

Mom, Dad, and Jackson appeared at the top of the stairs.

"How do you like it?" Dad asked.

"It's nice," I said with a smile. "I don't know if I'll be able to stand you people after the two weeks are up, but it's not too bad."

"Aw, you'll probably be sad once we arrive in Sitka and you have to leave the boat!" he said.

"Where are we staying in Sitka?" Jackson asked.

"Remember?" Dad asked. "Jim is letting us stay in their summer home on Halibut Point Road."

"Halibut Point Road? That's a weird name." Jackson wrinkled up his nose. "I hope it doesn't smell like fish. I hate fish."

Dad shook his head. "It's just a name. Besides, we will be eating lots of fish on the trip, so you'd better learn to love it."

Jackson made barfing noises and squeezed past us down the stairs. I took that as my cue to go upstairs and work my way out to the deck. I headed up to the bow and sat down, taking in the sunshine.

I closed my eyes and listened to the water lapping against the side of the boat and the call of the seagulls. I barely noticed that my mom had joined me until her leg brushed against mine.

"I have a surprise for you and Jackson," she said.

"You do?"

"I called Jim and asked him what the local kids do for fun during the summer."

"And?" I asked.

"Besides hunting and fishing, there is a really great summer camp called 'Sitka Fine Arts Camp.' So, I signed both of you up. You'll make some friends and hopefully have some fun."

"Mom, that's really sweet of you and everything, but I'm not that great of an artist. Jackson's pretty good, but I can barely draw a stick figure."

"Oh, but that's the best part!" She smiled. "It's not just art; it's theatre, dance, and music. You can pick whatever you want."

"I don't know. It sounds like I'll be too busy to call Mike every day. I don't like that."

She put her arm around my shoulders and hugged me closely. "I'm sure you'll have some time to chat with Mike."

I couldn't wait to see him. He had only been on his trip for a few days, but it seemed like a whole year had passed.

I got up and held my hand out to my mom, helping her up. "Come on. Let's get off the boat before Dad starts talking about how many knots the boat can travel."

Mom laughed. "You read my mind."

We climbed down the outside ladder to the dock and walked toward the parking lot.

"Hey!" Dad called out to us. "I wanted to show you the electric windlass!"

I grabbed Mom's hand, and we ran down the length of the dock, giggling all the way.

Chapter 10

On Wednesday, after class, Benny and I headed to the French bakery again. As we approached the sandwich board listing the daily specials, we caught sight of Frank heading toward us.

"Hey, kids." He pushed his glasses back up onto the bridge of his nose. "Are you going in?"

"Yeah." I opened the door. "Would you like to join us?"

"Sure—if you don't mind having an old codger along."

"We'd love to have you," I said as we filed in.

After we picked up our orders, we found a table near the window. It was a hot day, and the scent of fresh pastries and bread intensified in the warm air. I inhaled a deep breath, savoring the richness of the aromas.

"So," Frank said, sipping his black coffee. "What do you two think of the class so far?"

"It's good," both Benny and I said at the same time, and then laughed.

"Frank, I've been meaning to ask you..." I set down my iced tea. "Are you taking the class just to help you open up, or are you truly psychic?"

Benny gave me a sideways glance.

Frank's eyebrows shot upward. "Are you always this direct? I expected a little chit-chat before jumping in with the serious questions, little lady."

Oh, God, I'd made an ass out of myself again. Crimson spread from my neck up. How could I be so stupid?

Frank guffawed loudly and slapped me on the back, causing me to nearly knock over my iced tea. People turned around to stare at us, and then went back to their conversations.

"I'm just messin' with you!"

I nodded, embarrassed to have taken him seriously.

"Actually, it's a little of both, Jenny. I think I've been psychic all along, but I just wrote it off to coincidences. As a military man, everything was concrete to me—you know, black and white. No grays."

That made sense to me. I'd spent my whole life pushing my gift away. It took a lot of energy to make things black and white, though. And after I accepted who I was, life with grays seemed a lot easier.

"Now that I'm trying to make myself better so I can search for my family, my psychic… awareness, I guess you would call it, is really developing."

"Do you think they'll take you back when you find them?" Benny asked quietly.

"That's a good question. I'm afraid I don't have an answer for that, but I sure hope so. In the meantime, I need to improve my social skills." It was Frank's turn to look embarrassed. "I need to spend more time with people so that when I do find my family, it'll be easier to talk to them. So if either of you want to go fishing sometime, I'd be more than happy to take you."

Benny set his iced mocha on the table. "Fishing?"

"I know, I know." Frank chuckled. "It probably sounds really boring to kids these days. But for me, it's really relaxing. I'm getting a little bored going by myself, though. I could use some company. And I could practice my social skills. Like, talking with someone other than myself."

"That's a really nice offer, Frank," I said. "But my parents are dragging my brother and me up to Alaska on a boat this summer. I won't be around for at least a month."

"Alaska?" He took another sip of his coffee. "What brings you up there?"

For some strange reason, I felt compelled to tell him the whole story about Callie Shoemaker and the creepy guy, Richard Grist. Frank and Benny stared at me in morbid fascination.

"My God!" Frank nearly shouted. "That is an amazing story."

Benny agreed. "I knew some of that stuff about Callie through school, but I had no idea that you were involved."

"Well, that's a relief." I let out a breath. "I was getting worried that this whole thing would be leaked to the rest of the students, and then to the media."

Benny shook his head. "Not that I'm in the know or anything, but I didn't hear a thing about you."

Frank finished his coffee and leaned back in his chair. "Where in Alaska are you going?"

"Sitka."

"I've been there," Frank said. "Beautiful town. Good fishing."

I explained how Callie's dad had called and offered to take us up there and invited us to stay in his vacation home there.

"Sounds like a really nice trip, Jenny," he said.

I saw a hint of sadness in his eyes and felt the emptiness—a hole in his heart that only family could fill.

***

69

Friday rolled along all too soon. This was the last day of class, and I had to admit I was going to miss it when it was over.

Celine entered the room, smiling. She was wearing jeans, a cream tunic with embroidered trim belted at the waist, and a pair of brown sandals. Her curly, light brown hair was swept back and secured with a clip. A few tendrils had escaped and softly framed her face.

"It's Friday. You know what that means?" she asked, her eyes twinkling.

We shook our heads.

"It means it's field trip day!"

A couple of people laughed.

"I'm serious," she said. "We're going to walk down to Pioneer Square."

"Pioneer Square?" Frank asked. "What's in Pioneer Square? Besides all the drunks and bums, I mean."

"Ghosts," Celine answered simply. She laughed merrily as our eyes widened in surprise. "Yes, you heard me right: ghosts. Pioneer Square has a lot of history. There are all kinds of ghosts there—Native Americans, sourdoughs, lumberjacks, ladies of the evening, victims of the Great Fire. It should be interesting."

"So, what's the point?" Frank asked bluntly. "We're just going so we can see a bunch of ghosts? I've got one hanging around my property—I see him every day. The novelty has pretty much worn off for me."

Benny snickered, and I elbowed him.

"It's mostly for you to get a feel of the place," Celine answered. "I want you to feel the ghosts. Which ones are benevolent? Which ones have dark energy and should be avoided? If you come back for classes during the school year, and you develop your abilities more, I will teach you some psycho pomp work. But that's not until your third or fourth year."

"What's psycho pomp work?" I asked.

"That's a ritual of sorts. We do this to help spirits who are trapped here to cross over to the other side."

"What about the dark spirits?" another student asked.

"We tell them that they need to move on and to leave the area."

"Do they leave?" Benny asked.

"Sometimes," Celine answered. "And sometimes they come back."

"Creepy," I whispered.

"So, let's get started!" Celine clapped her hands. "I hope you've all worn comfortable shoes. It's a bit of a walk."

***

As we approached Pioneer Square, I heard a faint drumming sound. Bum ba ba bum bum. Bum ba ba bum bum.

We passed a tiny tourist shop crammed full of t-shirts, post cards, and Space Needle figurines. "I wonder if they have some sort of entertainment there today."

"What?" Benny looked puzzled.

"The drumming. Don't you hear it?"

"Uh, no," Benny looked at me as though I was crazy.

Bum ba ba bum bum. It was getting louder.

I narrowed my eyes at him. "You've got to be kidding. You don't hear that?"

"No." He shook his head.

When we arrived in the plaza, the drumming faded. There was the usual hustle and bustle of tourists and a multitude of pigeons. A little boy chased after one, his arms outstretched, a look of sheer delight on his face.

"Jaden, I told you not to chase them!" His exasperated mother ran after him and nearly twisted her ankle on the red cobblestones. "Those things are filthy. Blech!"

71

I laughed as the pigeon dodged just out of the boy's reach.

Celine waved her arm up in the air so we could see her. "Class, let's meet over here by the totem pole."

We crowded around her in a circle, scraping our legs against the low wrought iron fence and concrete planters. The leaves of the trees surrounding the totem cast us in dappled shade.

"Let's all say a little prayer here, in this place of power, and then get started."

I almost giggled as I said my own silent prayer. *Dear God, please don't let the birds on the branches above poop on my head.*

We closed our eyes and Celine said, "Spirit, we are here to learn. Show us the souls who are trapped in this space. Let these beautiful students see for themselves all who dwell in the in-between realm."

Celine turned to all of us and said solemnly, "Before you open your eyes, I want you to feel the energy within this place. Open your third eye. *Feel* it."

I breathed in, expanding my chest and then exhaled. As I opened my eyes, I heard the other students gasp. Why hadn't we seen this before?

There were people dressed in all kinds of old-fashioned clothing, as well as those who looked more modern. They seemed fairly solid to me, but you could just tell that they were ghosts. It was more of a feeling than anything else. A woman with dark, finger-waved hair, wearing too much rouge and lipstick, passed by us on the left. I could even hear her dress rustling about her legs as she sashayed across the plaza. A man with a handlebar moustache and a dapper hat nodded at me as he stepped across a grate on the uneven road. A fireman carrying a young child through the streets rushed by, his clothing covered in dark ashes, his face singed into a black, sooty blur.

Everywhere we looked, everywhere we turned, there were ghosts—dozens of them.

"Do you see?" Celine smiled. "Why don't you walk around and have a look? I just ask that you don't make it obvious. After all, there are plenty of *live* people around here that might think you're crazy if you do."

I moved uncertainly away from the totem, catching the eye of both Benny and Frank. They caught up to me and we continued further away from the group.

Benny laughed as we watched a horse and carriage roll by. "This is wild."

Frank put his arm out as the carriage passed, and it went right through him. He shivered, looking astonished.

I turned and saw a small group of Northwest Coastal Indian women hunched over some bushes, picking berries. They filled their woven cedar-strand baskets, juice dripping through the loose fibers.

Suddenly, a cold puff of air swirled around my shoulders, making the hair on the back of my neck stick straight up. I whipped my head around and caught a glimpse of a cloud of dark smoke. It circled Frank and then formed itself into a dark, menacing shape. It stopped right in front of him and opened its jaws wide, revealing a row of sharp yellow teeth.

"Aaah!" Frank yelped and jumped back.

Celine, who had been watching us nearby, rushed in and led us in a different direction.

"Never talk to spirits with teeth," she said in a hushed tone. "Just walk away."

My heart began beating again. Frank, Benny, and I exchanged panicked glances.

"What was that?" Benny asked.

"I don't know," Celine answered. "And I certainly don't want to find out."

We followed her back to the totem pole, and she waved her arms to get our group's attention.

"Did everyone have fun?" she asked. She seemed completely unfazed after the strange encounter just seconds ago.

Most of the students nodded in wonder. Frank and Benny raised their eyebrows, shaking their heads.

"We have lots to talk about when we get back to the classroom. Let's head on back and we can think about what we saw on the way," she said.

Some of the people seemed a little disappointed to be leaving so soon, but I was glad. That thing with teeth... I shuddered, thinking about what would've happened if Celine hadn't swooped in to save us.

As we left the square, the drumming started again. I glanced at the others in our group, but nobody seemed to notice it. I turned to look at the square and the totem. Suddenly, all the colors faded to black and white, as if I was looking at an old postcard. However, the people bustling about still looked modern. I sucked in a quick breath. What was happening?

The totem pole remained in color, like a bolt of lightning in a gray sky. I turned back to the group, now crossing the street and they too, were black and white. The drumming became louder and louder. My heart raced, matching the beat of the drum.

I followed behind the group, looking all around, trying to make sense of it all.

The drumming drowned out all of the other city noises around us.

But then I zeroed in on a voice coming toward our group. A man and a woman walked on the sidewalk, holding hands. They looked like any normal couple, except that the woman was in black and white, but the man was in full color. Why?

He was in his mid-fifties, with sandy blond hair graying at the temples. He was about twenty pounds overweight, and had a rounded nose. His outdated glasses were tinted dark from the sun. His khaki shorts hung to his knees and he was wearing socks and sandals.

I could hear him plain as day, but I couldn't hear what the woman was saying.

"So, I sold the house just last week," he said jovially. "Wish the economy was a little better. I should've gotten a lot more for it. Oh well!"

The woman said something, but all I could hear was the drumming.

"Well, it's not like we need the money." He laughed.

She laughed too. Or at least I think she did, and swung her Louis Vuitton handbag.

I turned to watch them pass as they headed to Pioneer Square, the totem's blazing color brightening as I stared.

Benny ran back and grabbed my arm.

"Hey! We almost left you behind. What are you staring at?"

I rubbed my eyes and looked at Benny—still black and white. I turned back to the couple, who were entering the plaza. Suddenly, several crows that had been sitting in the trees around the totem lifted out of the branches. Two or three of them dive-bombed the man and his girlfriend.

"Eeeeeee!" she shrieked, trying to fend them off with her bag.

The man looked utterly bewildered and covered his head with his arms.

"What the?" Benny muttered as he watched the man and woman.

Other people turned to stare, their mouths hanging open in shock. The crows flew higher, away from the crowd and headed north, cawing loudly. The drumming began in my ears again and increased in volume. I cringed, holding my hands over my ears.

Bum ba ba bum bum, bum ba ba bum bum.

The sound rushed through my ears, twisting and turning inside my head until I wanted to scream for mercy.

Benny wrapped an arm around me, shaking me gently. "Jenny?" his muffled voice called.

The drumming began to fade and then subsided. I took my hands off my ears and watched the couple, my heart beating out of my chest.

The crows were now small specks of black in the distance. I turned around and watched them continue their flight over the city. The buildings and sky slowly regained their color. I turned around again. The man and woman were brushing themselves off, shaking their heads. The onlookers had gone back to their shopping. Their color had returned as well.

Celine slipped in beside me. "Do you know what that was all about?"

I shook my head. "No."

"It had special meaning for you. The crows... did you notice them?"

I held her gaze and nodded slowly.

"Your symbols, Jenny. You must be careful."

Chapter 11

I woke up on Saturday morning, giddy with excitement. Mike was coming home tonight. The week that he had been gone had seemed like an eternity. I thought about the last night we had together... how close we'd become. I probably wouldn't be able to see him until Sunday, but I could hardly wait until then. I raced down the stairs and wolfed down a bowl of cereal.

Mom watched me in awe. "What on earth is up with you today?"

"I get to see Mike tomorrow," I said through a mouthful of cereal.

She watched me speed-chew my food. "So what's the big rush? You'll see him tomorrow."

"I know, but I've got to pack for the trip and run to the mall to buy him a present!"

Mom smiled, shaking her head. "Okay."

Obviously, she didn't get it. This was of monumental importance to me. I hadn't seen Mike in a whole week. And tomorrow was the only day I would be able to see him for an entire month. Everything had to be perfect.

I grabbed my empty bowl and quickly rinsed it in the sink, opened the dishwasher and shoved it in.

"Uh, Jenny?"

"Yup," I answered as I headed for the upstairs.

"Those were clean." She groaned.

"Huh?"

"The dishes. You just put a dirty dish in a dishwasher full of clean dishes."

"Oh, sorry!" I ran back, wrenched the door open, grabbed my dirty bowl and spoon and threw them in the sink.

She shook her head, a slight grin creeping across her face. "Go do your thing."

"Thanks!" I yelled as I took the stairs up to my room two at a time.

Once in my room, I hurriedly dressed in jeans, a t-shirt, and sneakers. What would I buy him? Nothing too extravagant, but it had to be meaningful. Something he could remember me by when I was away on my trip. I'd figure it out at the mall.

I grabbed my cell phone and shoved it into my pocket, flew down the stairs, and yelled goodbye to Mom as I jetted out the door.

"Bye, honey!" she called back as the door slammed shut.

I got in my Honda Civic, started the engine, and backed out of the driveway.

As I turned off of I-405 onto NE 8th to get to Bellevue Square Mall, traffic slowed to a crawl. What the heck? Then I saw the signs. The Bellevue Arts Fair was going on. Ugh, that was why there were so many people out and about. Maybe it would be fun to walk around and visit the booths. I might even find a present for Mike there.

I parked in the parking garage near Nordstrom's and then headed out around the sidewalk, and off to the arts fair.

***

The usual wind chimes, jewelry, and other kitschy items filled the booths this year. The warm sun beat down on me, making me smile. There was nothing better than a warm summer day, and this one was particularly delicious for some reason. I walked slowly past each vendor, trying to decide what to buy Mike. I wanted something meaningful. Something to tell him that… tell him what? I stopped dead in my tracks as the realization hit me. Something to tell him I *loved* him. Oh my God. That's what this feeling was. I was in love with Mike Kramer; really and truly, head-over-heels in love.

I laughed out loud and resisted the urge to twirl around with my arms stretched out wide in a kind of "the hills are alive with the sound of music" way. Why hadn't I known this earlier? It was such a revelation to me that I nearly floated as I started walking again.

In the very next booth sat a middle-aged woman with long black hair. She was selling Native American art— bracelets, earrings, hangings with bear and other animal symbols, and even some wooden boxes. I picked up a small square box, about two or three inches on each side. It was simple and elegant. I brushed the sides with my fingers, feeling how smooth and warm the wood was.

The lady nodded, a little smile passing over her lips. "That's a bentwood box."

"Bentwood?"

"It's a box made with cedar—it's all one piece of wood. The cedar is put in hot water and soaked until it bends. Then, it's shaped into a square and fastened together with wooden pegs. See how the edges are rounded?" She held one up and showing me the pegs. "Of course, the bottom is a separate piece and is also fastened to the sides with wooden pegs. Originally, they were made much bigger, but these are small—difficult to make."

I smiled and put down the little box. "They're beautiful."

She nodded. "Thank you, my husband makes them. He's Tlingit and learned how to make them from his grandfather."

"Tlingit?" I asked.

"That's a Native American tribe from Alaska."

"I'm going to Alaska in two days," I said, surprised. "We're taking a boat to Sitka."

The woman raised her eyebrows. "That's where my husband, Tommy, is from."

The coincidence was just too great. I had to have this for Mike—something to remember me by when I was on my trip.

I picked up another little box; one with a raven carved on the sides. The raven design was painted red and black while the top of the box was just natural wood. The art reminded me of the day we spent at Lincoln Park in West Seattle and the crows that had joined us for our picnic.

"This is perfect." I held it up for her to see. "I want to buy this for my boyfriend. How much?"

"It's two hundred," she replied.

"Oh." I set it back down on the table. "That's a little out of my price range."

"It's for your boyfriend?" Her warm brown eyes gazed at me curiously.

"Yes, he's coming back from his vacation tonight. I wanted to surprise him with something really special."

The woman smiled. "I remember what that was like. It's your first love, right?"

I nodded, savoring the word "love."

"Tell you what," she said. "How much cash do you have?"

Puzzled, I glanced at her to see if she was pulling my leg. A little smile crossed her lips, and she pointed at my purse.

I frowned and dug out my wallet. "I only have fifty dollars with me."

"Okay, then. How 'bout I let you have the box for fifty, and I'll even throw in this moonstone."

She held up a polished clear stone, carved in the shape of a heart. "Not only will he get this little box, but he'll get your heart as well."

Tears welled up in my eyes. She was so sincere. I had the perfect thing to give to Mike.

"Really?" I leaned forward and threw my arms around her. "Thank you!"

She pulled back, laughing. "I'm a sucker for true love."

I took out the cash I had in my purse and handed it to her. She wrapped the box and moonstone up in some tissue paper and placed it in a beautiful gift bag.

"Here you go, sweetie."

"Thank you so much." I took the bag and put it inside my purse. "Tell your husband thanks too. He's an amazing artist."

"I'll pass it on," she said.

I left the arts and crafts fair and walked back to the parking garage. I had to restrain myself from skipping back to my car. I was so excited. I couldn't wait to give the present to Mike, and I couldn't wait to tell him how I felt about him. Tomorrow was going to be the perfect day.

Chapter 12

I was all packed for the trip. Even though I was sad to leave, I could hardly wait to see Mike. I had rummaged through my closet to put together an outfit—a Mediterranean blue halter top to match my eyes and show off my tan shoulders, and a short, flirty, white skirt. I accessorized with a pair of delicate blue topaz earrings. Mike had called early in the morning, and we had made plans to have a picnic at Lake Boren Park.

I checked myself out in the bathroom before going downstairs. My cheeks were flushed, and I practically radiated happy energy. I had used a flat iron to straighten my already straight blonde hair into a silky curtain. My make-up was applied sparingly, but at the last minute I added a pale pink gloss to my lips.

The doorbell rang. I took a deep breath and left the bathroom, slowly making my way down the stairs. Mom answered the door, and Mike was standing there, looking like the most handsome guy in the universe. He was tan, and his brown hair had honey-colored streaks woven into it by the sun. My mom and Mike turned to watch me come down the stairs. I felt like a princess making her debut at a ball.

His green eyes lit up when he saw me. Both Mom and Mike uttered, "Wow!" as I quickly went down the rest of the stairs.

"I missed you so much!" I threw myself into his arms. He wrapped them around me and kissed me.

A surge of electricity flowed through my body as our lips touched. I stood on tiptoe and looked into his eyes and grinned. The corner of his lips drew up slightly, as if he was amused at my enthusiasm.

"Miss me much?" he asked slyly.

My mom watched us, and shook her head with a smile. "Well, you two, I'll leave you alone. Jenny, be sure to be back by six o'clock. We're having an early dinner. We'll be up at the crack of dawn tomorrow morning."

I fought the urge to roll my eyes. "Okay, Mom."

The last thing I wanted was to go to bed early. I just wanted to spend the evening with my dream guy.

Mom retreated to the kitchen, and Mike leaned down to whisper, "You look gorgeous."

"So do you. I can't take my eyes off you."

He put his arm around me kissed the top of my head.

"Ready for our picnic?" He turned the door knob.

"Of course. Oh, wait! I almost forgot." I grabbed the gift bag from the table by the door.

"What's that?"

"Just a little something I picked up for you."

"You shouldn't have," he said. "I didn't get you anything… except for the food in the picnic basket in the car."

I laughed. "Food is always good. Besides, you're the best present I could have hoped for."

He squeezed my shoulder as we walked out the door.

***

We walked past Lake Boren, watching dragonflies darting around the lily pads. Songbirds filled the air with their music. I wrapped my arm around Mike's waist, inhaling his scent and leaning my head into his shoulder as we followed the path. We found a quiet, out-of-the-way spot in the park to spread out our blanket and picnic food. Mike unpacked the basket. He laid out turkey sandwiches, chips, potato salad, and two bottles of sparkling water.

"You really went all out. This looks yummy." I unwrapped my sandwich.

Mike shrugged. "It was no trouble at all."

I took a bite and grinned at him, hoping that I didn't have lettuce stuck in my teeth. My insides were all tangled up in a knot. I wanted to tell him how I felt, but it seemed awkward to just bring it up out of the blue. Maybe I would just start a conversation and bring up my feelings somehow.

"You have to tell me all about your trip." I took a sip of my water.

"It was good. We sailed, we fished... you know, that was about it."

"That was it? Did you like your dad's boss and his wife? Were you bored?" I asked. A little ant trekked across the blanket and headed for my leg. I flicked it across the grass, and it started its journey all over again.

"Yeah, they were nice. I wasn't that bored, really—I listened to music, read books. It was good to relax. I missed you, though."

Was it my imagination or did he seem sad? Perhaps he wanted to tell me about his feelings for me. I took this as a cue to bring it up. "Mike," I said, reaching for the gift bag I had set beside the picnic basket, "I wanted to give you something."

He looked into my eyes, a faint smile forming on his lips. Taking the bag from me, he reached in and drew out the little box. He turned it around in the palm of his hand. "What's this?"

My stomach did a couple of flips. I had to get the courage up to say it.

"It's a... a... bento box," I answered.

Mike laughed lightly. "A bento box? Is there sushi in there?"

Oh my God.

"Ah geez, I mean it's a bentwood box." My faced burned with embarrassment. "It's made by a Native American artist from Sitka."

"Sitka? Where you are going on vacation?" he asked.

"Yes. I wanted to get you something that would remind you of me while I was gone. The raven design reminded me of that day in Lincoln Park in West Seattle. You know, with the crows?"

"Oh." He nodded. "I remember that."

I swallowed. "Open... open the box."

He carefully opened the lid, peeked inside, and then pulled out the heart-shaped moonstone.

"It's a heart." I instantly realized that I was stating the obvious.

"Yes, I see that." His mouth twitched, and he looked down.

There it was again. He definitely seemed sad and a little uncomfortable. Did he know what I was going to say?

"So, the stone," I went on, hesitating, "uh... it symbolizes—um, I... uh."

"What?"

I laughed nervously. "Well, when I leave, I'll leave my heart with you. Because... because... I love you, Mike. I'm in love with you."

I did it! I told him! I looked into his eyes, waiting for his response; waiting to see what his reaction would be.

His face was ashen—he looked stunned. Oh, God. Did I scare him? Maybe I should've waited to tell him.

He leaned forward and hugged me, patting my back.

"Thank you, Jenny," he murmured. "That's very sweet."

Very sweet? I pulled back from him and searched his face for reassurance, a warm smile... anything.

"Mike?" I asked.

He bit his lip, and looked away.

Dread seeped into my heart.

He finally looked at me. "Jenny, on my trip, I had a lot of long talks with my dad's boss. He stressed the importance of uh—the need for focus in college; particularly the first year. He told me that the first year set the tone for your whole academic experience."

"Uh huh."

"And he also talked about how having a career in the performing arts can be unpredictable. I could end up being a waiter my whole life just waiting to be cast in a Broadway show or a movie."

I looked at him apprehensively, not comprehending where this was going.

"So, he convinced me to get a second major in business. That way, I would have something to fall back on. My dad thought it was a good idea too."

I still didn't understand why he looked so pale and what this had to do with me.

"When I told him about you, about how great you are and how much I cared for you, he reminded me again about focus."

I shook my head. "I don't understand. Did he tell you not to date me anymore?"

His nod was so imperceptible, if I hadn't been staring at him, I wouldn't have noticed it.

"What did you tell him?" I asked.

"I told him that I felt strongly about you. But he and my dad made a really great case as to why I shouldn't get serious with *any* girl. I realized he was probably right. That

86

I really should focus—but that doesn't mean that I don't have feelings for you!" he said with a panicked look.

He reached out to take my hand. I pulled away. "I really want to be your friend, and have you be a part of my life. But probably no more than that for the first year—until I get a good grip on studying and getting through my classes."

"I can't believe what I'm hearing." Tears filled my eyes. "You don't want to be with me?"

"I do! It's just that I won't have enough time to be a good boyfriend to you. But I don't want to lose you." He moved closer to me.

I pushed away from him, my palms slamming into his chest so that he had to catch his balance.

"You're breaking up with me, but you want to be with me? That doesn't make any sense. My God—I just told you that I'm in love with you. I'm so stupid!"

My voice caught in my throat. I felt like I could barely breathe. My heart was practically pounding its way out of my chest. Anger, pain, humiliation... all those feelings coursed through me at once.

I picked up the box and threw it across the grass where it landed in a clump of bushes. And then I ran. I didn't even glance back at him when he yelled, "Jenny! Jenny, please come back. Let me explain!"

I sobbed as I fled. How did this happen? I had never felt this way about anyone before. Every part of me was in love with him. Hurt and rejection stabbed my heart as I stumbled through an unmarked path, blackberry vines scratching at my legs. I winced as my foot caught on a tree root and twisted beneath me. I hitched in a sob and fell to my knees, my white skirt now streaked with dirt. I got up, tested my ankle, and ran on. I reached the pipeline trail, where it was wide enough for the natural gas trucks to move through, but no other cars were allowed. I knew he couldn't follow me there. Even if he drove down Coal

Creek Parkway where the trail ended, I knew he wouldn't find me.

I ran and ran, not caring about the concerned faces of passersby, not feeling my legs or my feet. When I got to the pavement, I increased my pace. I had never been a long distance runner, especially in sandals, and my body was complaining. My lungs felt like they would burst from the workout I was forcing on them. A car honked as I bolted across the street.

How could he do this to me? I loved him!

I ran past the shopping center, my feet pounding the pavement. Why did he have to listen to his dad?

As soon as I reached the intersection to Forest Drive, I took a right and began the climb up the hill. The muscles in my thighs were burning, and I compelled them to transport me up the steep incline.

Why didn't he want me? Why couldn't he love me back?

In one last heroic effort before my body failed me, I turned up my street. I had expended every ounce of energy I could afford. Finally, I reached my house, soaked in sweat, my face streaked with tears. I wrenched open the front door, catapulted up the stairs and into my room, slammed the door, and threw myself onto the bed.

"Jenny?" my mom yelled from downstairs. "Jenny, what's wrong?"

I pulled the pillow over my head and shut out the rest of the world.

Chapter 13

"Jenny, wake up, honey. It's time to leave for the harbor." Mom gently shook me awake.

I forced my eyes open and groaned. My body was on fire, every muscle aching and complaining.

She was kneeling down by the side of my bed, her face lined with worry. "Look, honey, I know something happened between you and Mike yesterday. Remember, I tried talking to you about it?"

I didn't remember anything beyond my own misery.

"You said a few things about Mike, but I couldn't really understand your words, you were crying so hard."

I grimaced and closed my eyes again. I just wanted to sleep.

"It's going to be okay, sweetie, you just need a little time to get over this." She brushed the hair off my cheek.

I shook my head. I wasn't ready to speak yet.

"Come on, why don't you take a shower? The warm water will calm you. Besides, you won't get many showers while we are on the boat. This will be the last one you'll get for several days."

Ugh. The friggin' boat. I groaned and opened my eyes again.

"Do I have to go?" I croaked. My throat felt like sandpaper.

"You sound terrible. And yes, you have to go." Mom pulled back my covers. "Let's get you out of bed and get a drink of water."

She helped me up and led me to the bathroom. As she filled the glass by the sink, I caught a glimpse of myself in the mirror. Oh my God. I looked like a boiled lobster with blonde hair. My face was red, my eyes were slits surrounded by tear-soaked skin. Yech.

"Do you want to talk about it?" Mom looked at my reflection.

I shook my head.

"Okay, but if you want to talk, I'll be downstairs. Take a nice shower, and you'll feel better." She hugged me and left the room.

***

Somehow, I got through the shower and breakfast and now sat glumly in the back of our SUV as we drove to the harbor.

Jackson looked at my still puffy face and furrowed his brow. "What happened to you? Had a run-in with a tractor trailer? Or maybe walked into a wall? You look horrible."

"Jackson," my mom said sharply. "You leave Jenny alone. She and Mike broke up."

Jackson rolled his eyes when Mom turned back around. He whispered, "Lover boy dumped you, huh?"

I glared at him and jammed my elbow into his side.

"Ow! Jenny hit me!" he yelped.

"Jackson, knock it off," my dad growled.

"But…"

"Stop it, right now," Dad warned.

I slunk down into my thick hoodie and hugged my arms tightly around me. I just wanted to sleep and make the hurt go away. The pain was far worse than any injury I had ever had… and I'd had my fair share of physical injuries. The emotional hurt occupied my every cell. I wanted to pick up the phone and call my best friends, but Aya and Julia were at their cheerleading camp in California. Hannah was still on vacation, too. I felt so alone.

***

I was out of it as we loaded all of our supplies onto the boat. My body went through the motions of handing boxes and bags to my dad and Jim, who were standing on deck.

Why did Mike have to break up with me right before my trip?

"Jenny," Dad said softly. "Why don't you go ahead and take a break. We can handle the rest of this."

I went down to the room I was sharing with Jackson. I unrolled my sleeping bag, crawled onto my bunk, and pulled my pillow over my head. The trip was going to take a couple of weeks. I had no idea if I could survive that long.

Several hours later I heard footsteps.

"Jenny?" my mom whispered.

"Yeah," I groaned.

"I brought you something to eat."

Food. Come to think of it, I was hungry. I had only picked at my breakfast, pushing my food around the plate. I hadn't eaten dinner the night before either... or lunch for that matter. I had only taken one bite of sandwich before Mike dropped the break-up bomb on me. The memory washed over me again, making me feel even worse.

I sat up and Mom sat beside me on my bunk. She held the plate out to me: a cup of chicken noodle soup, saltine crackers, and some grapes.

"I've got a can of lemon-lime soda for you too," she said, handing it to me. "It should help to settle your stomach."

My eyes filled with tears. "Thanks, Mom," I sniffed. "You're the best."

"I remember what it feels like to have a broken heart." She put her arm around me.

I sniffled. "I just don't understand it. I thought that he cared about me."

"Oh honey, I'm sure he does care about you. Did he tell you why?"

I explained about Mike's talks with his dad and his dad's boss.

"Ah—that makes sense," she said.

"What? How can you defend him?"

"I don't agree with what he did, honey," she answered, "but it makes sense that he went along with what his dad wanted. He's a good guy. He respects his parents' opinion. But sometimes, parents can be wrong. He just needs a little more maturity to be able to stand up to his father."

"Are you saying that he should go against what his dad wants?"

"Yes, I do. Because at eighteen, he can make his own decisions. It's not like he's some kind of juvenile delinquent who takes drugs and rides his skateboard all day. He's a good kid."

"Do you think he'll want me back someday?" I sniffed.

"I don't know, honey. Maybe. Maybe not. I know you don't want to hear this right now, but there are a lot of other fish in the sea. In time, you'll find someone who loves you, and treats you the way you deserve to be treated."

"In other words, you don't think he'll want me back, right?" I hitched in a breath, feeling the tears start to well up again.

"All I'm saying is that he may or may not come around. Don't spend your time pining for someone who doesn't reciprocate your feelings or fight for you."

I wiped the tears off my face, even as more were leaking out.

The cell phone in my pocket buzzed. I dug it out and looked at the number. I swallowed hard. It was Mike. I glanced up at my mom, sniffed, and then turned the ringer off. It was over.

Chapter 14

I had no idea what day it was—or even if it was day. It could have been night for all I knew. I was only aware of the endless bobbing up and down, and being cradled by the waves.

Finally, I emerged out of my cocoon and unzipped my sleeping bag. Filtered light from the hall faintly illuminated our room. Jackson was sacked out on his bunk, his arm hanging off the edge of the mattress, a dried bit of drool stuck in the corner of his mouth. Yuck.

Quietly, I crept up the stairs to the main room with the galley and table. I slipped out the door and onto the deck.

Green.

Everything was green. We were anchored in a cove with a little beach on its shore. The trees on the island reflected their color into the water, the gentle waves lapping quietly onto the sand.

No one else was awake. I tiptoed to the bow and sat down cross-legged, pulling my arms tightly around me and hugging myself. I took the phone out of my pocket. No battery. I frowned and tucked it back in.

A crow swooped down from a tall fir tree and sat on the railing of the boat. It eyed me critically, as if to say, "Where were you?"

"I was dying a slow death downstairs," I whispered hoarsely to him.

Geez—what was up with crows? They seemed to follow me wherever I went. Then I remembered what Celine had told me when she saw my collage board in class.

"The raven, a harbinger of death or a bad omen."

Did this mean that I was going to be the one to die on a boat? At first, I had thought that Mike would be the one in danger, but his boat trip was over now. He was safe and sound, getting ready to go to college, and start his new life without me. A wave of anger and sadness washed over me, and my eyes welled up with tears.

Caw! The crow startled me back to the present.

It cocked its head to the side, and then hopped up from the railing and landed on my left shoulder. I froze.

I sat rigidly, barely daring to breathe.

Flash.

The boat was on fire. I was in the water, numb with the cold. A scream pierced the night—so shrill and filled with fear it took my breath away.

Boom!

Sections of boat and debris flew through the air and splashed all around me. A huge jagged piece of wood glided through the blackness, showering sparks into the air before it hit me.

I gasped. The crow suddenly lifted off my shoulder and flew up and along the shoreline. My hands were trembling as I brought them up to my mouth in horror.

My heart pounded so loudly, I thought it would wake up everyone on the boat.

Damn. This could only mean one thing. This boat was going to burn, and we were going to die. Waking people up wasn't a bad idea. They had to know about this. I got up hurriedly and nearly tripped over a coiled rope in my haste to alert my mom and dad. I steadied myself and rushed

95

inside. I made my way to their bedroom and shook Mom's shoulder.

Her eyes snapped open. She clapped her hand over her heart and gasped. "Oh my God, Jenny! You scared me to death. What's wrong?"

Dad snorted and rolled over.

"We have to get off this boat," I hissed.

"What? Why?"

"I think we are in real danger," I said urgently.

Mom sat up and pushed the covers to the side. She grabbed a fleece jacket from the hook on the wall and escorted me up the stairs and into the galley. Motioning for me to sit down at the table, she joined me and leaned forward, her elbows on the smooth teak surface.

"What's this all about?" she whispered.

I told her about the vision.

"I've had this same vision like three or four times now," I said. "I keep getting bits and pieces of it and frankly, it scares me to death."

Mom took in the information, concern wrinkled her forehead.

"I remember you telling me about this before Dad announced that we were taking a boat to Alaska. Obviously, it wasn't about Mike."

"Yeah, and we're the only people I know on a boat trip. It has to be about us."

"I don't know," she said slowly. "What if it's not?"

"Then why would I keep having these visions? Over and over?"

Jim walked into the galley and yawned. "I heard talking, is anything wrong?" He pulled the kettle out of a cupboard.

I exchanged a nervous glance with Mom.

Mom hesitated for a moment and then said, "Actually, since you know about Jenny's gift, I think it's safe to tell you. She's been having some disturbing visions and woke me up to warn me."

"Your gift saved my daughter's life, so I'm all ears. What did you see?" He filled the kettle, placed it on the tiny stove top, and turned it on.

"Well, I keep having a vision of a boat exploding," I said quietly.

He furrowed his brow and sat down at the table across from me.

"A boat exploding? Tell me more." His brown eyes watched me intently.

I talked in great detail, piecing together all of the visions I'd had about the boat since they had started.

"So, you think that *this* is the boat that will explode?"

I blew out a breath and nodded.

He smiled.

"You don't believe me, do you?" I said indignantly.

"No, no, it's not that." He shook his head. "I'm smiling because an explosion is very unlikely on this boat."

"What do you mean?" my mom asked.

"This boat has a diesel engine. It's not a spark-ignition engine like those that are fueled by gas. It uses the heat of compression to ignite it."

Mom and I looked at him, our faces blank.

He laughed. "I guess I didn't explain it that well. In simpler terms, there is no spark when it engages the ignition. And no spark means that there's no chance that it will catch on fire and explode. Heck, even the stove is electric—not gas. So, no worries about open flames."

"Oh," both Mom and I said at the same time.

My face reddened. "Well, I feel dumb now."

"No need to feel dumb," he said with a grin. "I guess only people who know engines would know that."

I was frustrated. "So, why do I keep having these visions?"

97

He shrugged. "I'm sure you'll figure it out and maybe it will help someone or keep them safe."

"He's probably right," Mom said. "It's best not to worry about it for now. No sense in making yourself sick over something you have no control over."

No control. Story of my life lately.

The kettle whistled, and Jim got up and set out three mugs. He opened some Starbucks instant coffee packets and dumped them into each cup.

"Do you ladies like your coffee black or with cream and sugar?"

"Cream and sugar," Mom and I answered in unison.

I didn't drink much coffee, but now I thought I needed it. I had a lot of sorting out to do in my mind. I cupped my hands around the mug as Jim handed it to me. I took a sip. The warmth trickled down my throat and comforted me from the inside out.

Dad shuffled into the galley, ruffling his hair with one hand. He yawned. "Why are you all up so early?"

Jim made more coffee and handed a cup to my dad. "Jenny keeps having premonitions of exploding boats. I told her that it was extremely unlikely that this boat would explode because it has a diesel engine."

"Oh, yeah." Dad nodded. "Heat compression instead of spark ignition."

Boat nerds.

I'd had enough of the engine talk.

"Do you mind if I go outside for a bit?" I slid out of the cushioned bench.

"Sure, go ahead." Dad took my place at the table. "We'll make some breakfast and call you when it's done."

I went outside to the bow and sat down with my coffee in hand. I took another sip. These visions were driving me nuts. They were not going to go away until the explosion happened. I still wasn't getting enough information to do anything about it.

I scooted forward closer to the edge of the boat, and stared down into the water. I wished I had charged my phone so I could at least talk to my friends. Aya and Julia were back from cheerleading camp by now. Hannah was probably home from her vacation too. Madeline was doing a play at Youth Theatre Northwest. I felt a pang of guilt, wishing that I had called her before I left for Alaska.

My mind wandered to thoughts of Mike. What was he doing now?

Flash.

Mike's bedroom.

He was lying on his side. I was on his bed snuggled up next to him.

"Jenny," he murmured in his sleep.

I wriggled even closer to him.

He reached over and ran his fingers through the fur on my neck.

I licked his arm and a smile crept across his face. His eyes opened a crack.

"How did you get up here, you little rascal?"

I blinked hard.

Green.

Trees.

Back on the boat.

What was that? I was sure for an instant that I was Kaya, Mike's dog.

Whoa. That had never happened before. I could see through an animal's eyes?

The shock wore off, and a new thought sprung into my head. He had said my name in his sleep. What did that mean? Maybe he still had feelings for me. I knew I could now tune into Kaya to keep tabs on him. Doubt crept into my mind. Was that ethical? How would I feel if it were the other way around? I wouldn't like it.

I took another sip of coffee. My eagerness to test my newly discovered skill overrode my sense of right and wrong. I tried to access Kaya again. I closed my eyes and thought about Mike.

Flash.

Outside in the yard.

I peed in the grass.

"Good girl," Mike praised.

I looked up at him and then looked down and noticed his shoelaces. I attacked them, pulling the string through my teeth.

"Stop that!" He laughed. "Come on girl, let's go inside."

Well, that was weird. So, it seemed that I could easily tune into Kaya. Could I do that with other animals?

"Jenny!" Dad called. "Breakfast!"

The smell of pancakes wafted out of the cabin and my stomach grumbled noisily. I resolved to try my experiment with other animals later.

Chapter 15

After breakfast, everyone got dressed and went out onto the deck.

"We're only about two hours away from Bedwell," Jim said. "We'll need to stop there and go through Canadian Customs."

Jackson wrinkled up his nose. "What's Customs?"

"It's the border between the U.S. and Canada. We'll have to present our passports to the officials. They'll ask us questions and hopefully let us go on our way," Jim explained.

"Like when we went to Mexico a couple of years ago? But it's only Canada. Why do we need passports?"

I looked at him, my mouth hanging open. "Seriously, Jackson?"

"What?" He glared at me.

"Canada is a foreign country. What are they teaching you in school?" I smirked.

"Hey!" he said as he swung at me. "I know Canada is a different country. I just didn't think it was foreign *enough* to need passports."

I stepped back, avoiding his fist.

"Control yourself, dude." I snorted.

"Jackson," my mom warned. "Do not hit your sister."

"But she practically called me an idiot," he whined.

"No, she didn't. She just thought you knew about needing passports. And Jenny, not long ago, you didn't need passports to enter Canada."

"Whatever," I said under my breath.

Mom threw her arms up in the air. "Can't you two get along for once?"

Jackson rolled his eyes and stomped off into the cabin.

I made my way to the front of the vessel and sat down on my new favorite place, the bow. With Jackson and I in such close quarters, I wasn't sure I'd live long enough to make it to Alaska. Maybe the boat would explode first before I throttled the little brat. No, the boat would not explode—or so the boat nerds said.

The engines started up, and we slowly turned out of the cove and meandered up along the coastline. Gulls called to each other as they flew overhead. I took in a deep breath and let it out, my body relaxing as I watched the water churning at the tip of the bow.

Flash.

"Okay, Devon, I'll be gone for a couple of days. You'll be fine here on your own, won't you?"

"You're... you're leaving me here all by myself?" I asked, trembling.

"I told you, it's fine," the man said sharply. "I have to work a double shift. You want food on the table, don't you?"

He got in the boat, started it up, and pulled away from the tiny dock.

I threw myself on the rocky beach and sobbed.

I snapped back to my reality. Oh, no. Devon. I wracked my brain. What information could I pass on to Detective Coalfield?

He was on a small island. The bad guy, his dad, had to take a boat to work. This would be easy! All I had to do was tell the detective that Devon was living at his dad's house on an island. I reached for my phone. Ugh, I hadn't had a chance to recharge it. Damn it.

I got up from my perch on the bow and made my way to the cabin. Jackson was slumped on the cushions at the table. I ignored him and went downstairs to my sleeping area. I dug my charger out of my bag, and plugged it into the outlet.

I ran back upstairs. Mom had entered the cabin while I was downstairs and was sponging off the counter top next to the stove.

"Can I borrow your phone?" I asked.

"Why don't you use yours?"

"Out of juice."

She took her phone out of her pocket. "Here you go."

I turned it on. No bars.

I squeezed my eyes shut and handed it back to her.

"No reception out here, huh?" Mom tucked her phone away. She picked up the sponge and wrung it dry in the sink.

I shook my head. "I'll try again when we get to the Customs office."

I wondered why I was getting so many visions all stacked on top of each other. First the boat explosion, then the doggy visions, and now flashes of Devon. I gritted my teeth. This was getting out of control.

***

"Welcome to Poet's Cove!" Jim shouted to us as we congregated on deck.

A massive resort rose out of the wooded shore; it stair-stepped up a slight incline, making it seem even larger than it really was. It was nestled so nicely into the terrain that it looked like it had always been a part of the landscape.

"This is the Canadian Customs office?" I asked, wide-eyed.

Jim laughed. "Well, sort of. The lodge is called Bedwell Resort. It's a great place to spend a few days to relax. It's got a pool, a spa, and everything. But if you look over there, you'll see Customs." He carefully steered the boat closer to the pier.

The office was perched on wooden pilings, hovering above the marina. A long ramp led from the dock to the office.

"Why didn't we spend the night here instead of on the boat?" Jackson frowned at Jim.

"Because we would have had to travel two hours in the dark to get here. I don't like to take risks like that," Jim answered.

"Hmmph!" Jackson walked over to the rail and looked at the marina. "Can we at least get off the boat and look around?"

"Sure," Jim said. "We can treat ourselves to an early lunch at the Aurora Restaurant. But first we'll need to visit Customs."

Mom went back into the cabin and grabbed a thick manila folder off the table.

"I've got all our information here." She closed the cabin door behind her and stood next to me on the deck.

"Actually, the skipper—that's me, and head of the household—that's you," Jim said pointing at my dad, "need to go into the office first. Once we're cleared, they'll come to the boat and look through the children's passports and yours too. You guys stay put while we go do that."

Jim steered the boat to the Customs dock and expertly lined it up in one of the slips. Dad jumped off and grabbed the rope and tied it to the cleat. Jim nimbly hopped off the boat and they made their way to the office.

When they came back with the official, we got to our feet to greet them. The older man sat down at the table and sifted through all of the papers. After some general chit-chat and questions, he gave us the all-clear and left.

"We have to move the boat to the other dock," my dad told us. Jim hopped back into the captain's seat and started the boat.

"Why?" Mom asked.

"This dock is only for people checking in with Customs. We need to dock over there." He pointed at the dock nearby. There were only a few spots open.

Everyone was antsy and ready to be on land. It had only been a day and a half and we were already feeling cooped up. I suddenly remembered my cell phone, and whipped into the cabin and down the stairs to snatch it out of the charger.

By the time I got back to the deck, everyone was already halfway to the shore. I climbed off the boat and caught up to them.

"Any chance we can all get a shower here?" Mom asked Jim.

"Sure. Let's get a bite to eat first, and then we can get cleaned up."

***

After we had lunch and took showers, I walked up to the coffee shop. The rest of the family had gone for a short walk to stretch their legs.

The familiar smell of brewed coffee and the sweet aroma of pastries made me feel like I had suddenly rejoined civilization. I breathed in a deep whiff of mocha-scented air, ordered a hot drink, and pulled my phone out of my pocket. I was anxious to call the detective and relay the info from my recent vision.

"Chai Latte!" the barista called out. I took it from her and smiled in thanks. I sat down and made a call.

"Detective Coalfield," he answered on the first ring.

"Hi, it's Jenny."

"Jenny, great to hear from you. Where are you?"

"We just went through Customs in Canada; we're in Poet's Cove."

"Poet's Cove! I love that place," he said. "So, what do you have for me?"

"I had another vision about Devon. He was on a little island and his dad had to take a boat to work. So, if you get his dad's address, you should find him."

"Little island?"

"Yeah, in the vision, it seemed like it was off the mainland or something," I answered.

"Huh. That's weird. His father's house is on Baranof, but that island is really large."

Baranof? Where had I heard that name before?

"Detective, is Baranof also the name of the town he lives in?"

"No, the name of the town is Sitka."

"Sitka?" I said loudly. Several people turned to stare at me.

"Yes. Is something wrong?" he asked.

"No," I said, lowering my voice, "but that's where we are going."

"You're going to Sitka?" he asked. "What a coincidence!"

"This is no coincidence, Detective. Now I understand why I was having all these visions of Devon."

"Oh, wow," he said slowly. "So..."

"Someone is leading me to him."

Chapter 16

We had made some progress, traveling at eight knots all day. Eight knots is painfully slow, but we had motored steadily, and had made our way up the narrow straits safely; though I could tell it was challenging to navigate them. By the time we anchored, the images of tranquil coves, glassy water, and shores with rock-strewn beaches had become commonplace.

While continuously mulling over my visions of Devon, I had come to the conclusion that I was meant to find him. The thought terrified me because Devon's father, Vince McLeod, was clearly insane. Detective Coalfield had promised he would contact the Sitka Police Department to let them know about me. I hoped they wouldn't think we were both crazy.

Mom had bought a stash of cheesy Archie comic books at the gift shop. I was reading them leisurely on deck while chewing on my fourteenth stick of red licorice.

"I'm going in to make dinner," my mother said, eyeing the nearly empty box of candy. "You might want to stop snacking or you won't have room for real food."

I shrugged. "Okay."

The sun began sinking in the sky, painting the wispy clouds in purples and pinks. I listened to the sound of dishes clanking and pots bubbling while I watched the sky turn to an inky indigo.

Could the images of the boat explosion be related to the visions of Devon? They didn't seem to be linked, but maybe there was a piece of information I hadn't received yet that would somehow tie it all together.

"Jenny! Jackson!" Mom yelled.

I stacked the comic books together and tucked them under my arm. The smell of chili and cornbread seeped out of the door to the cabin. Dad held it open for me.

"Wait until you taste this, Jenny. Mom has outdone herself again."

If there was one thing my mom was especially good at, it was cooking. My stomach rumbled in anticipation.

Jackson came flying up the stairs. "What are we having?"

"Chili and cornbread," Mom said.

He wrinkled up his nose and sat down with his arms crossed.

"What's the matter, Jackson?" Jim asked. He buttered a piece of cornbread and took a bite. "Mary, this is outstanding!"

Jackson scooped a tiny bit of chili on his spoon and tasted it. I could tell he was starving because normally he wouldn't even bother to try it. He dipped his spoon in again.

My jaw dropped open. "He actually likes it!"

Perhaps my little brother was growing up.

***

After dinner, we all squeezed together on deck. Jim brought a couple of lanterns and set them out; the light reflected off the black water and twinkled like moonlight. Jackson went nosing around the deck in the front of the boat.

"What's he doing?" I asked.

"Oh, he's just exploring," Dad said.

"So, Jenny, anymore visions of boats exploding?" Jim asked.

I shook my head. "Not since this morning."

Jackson came back to the stern.

"Hey, Dad, what's this thing?" He held an orange stick up for us to see. The end of it came dangerously close to the glowing lantern.

In the split second it took for me to figure out that it was a flare, I jumped to my feet.

"Jackson, no!" my dad yelled, but to me it was as if it was in slow motion. The sound waves lowered the pitch of Dad's voice, so it came out more like, "Jaaaccckkksssooon, nooooo!"

An image of a burning boat flashed before my eyes. I didn't hesitate. I launched myself toward Jackson. My fingers reached toward the flare.

Jackson's eyes widened in shock. I snatched the flare from his hand, and my body kept going, going—over the rail.

The cold water surged up to greet me, and I plunged into its darkness. Shock rattled my limbs and made my heart skip a beat. Above me, the lights of the lantern twinkled through the murkiness, the salt stinging my eyes.

"Jenny!" Mom screamed. Her voice muffled by the water swirling in my ears.

Splash!

Arms reached out, grabbing my hoodie, yanking me to the surface. Dad's strong arms pulled me through the dark water. He reached the ladder on the back of the boat, and pushed my body up to the rungs. Hands extended down and pulled me up first and then my father. I lay gasping on the wood, spluttering and shivering.

"Oh my God!" Mom shrieked.

"She's okay, Mary," Jim said. "Get Jenny and Pete a blanket."

She immediately tore off into the cabin.

Jim helped me to sit up. Water dripped off me in rivulets and ran down my shoulders and arms. The puddles pooled at my sides and shimmered like Christmas lights on a rainy night.

Dad scooted over next to me, and put his dripping arm around me. "Sweetheart, are you all right?"

I nodded. I looked up at his chin and wiped a drop of water from it. "What about you? Are you okay?"

"Of course. That was a close call, huh? At least we didn't blow up," he said.

Jackson knelt down in front of us. "Guys, I didn't know the orange stick was a flare."

"It's okay, Jackson. You didn't mean to put us in danger." Dad patted his back.

"Well, nobody died, so I guess everything is okay," Jackson announced. He got up from his crouch and went into the cabin.

I rolled my eyes.

Mom came out with two big bath towels. She quickly draped one around my shoulders and then a second around Dad's.

"I'm going to make some hot cocoa to warm you up," Jim said. He slipped into the cabin, leaving just the three of us on deck.

"I'm just glad those stupid visions will finally go away now. They were driving me nuts."

Mom laughed nervously. "Can you imagine if Jackson had just let the flare get a little closer to the lantern?"

"I *can* imagine it," I replied dryly. "I've been playing that scene in my head over and over again."

Dad tilted his head back and let out a bark of laughter. We stared at him for a moment, our eyes wide.

Mom stifled a giggle. She picked up the end of Dad's towel and rubbed his head affectionately. Suddenly, we all burst into laughter as the shock of the moment sunk in.

"Let's go in and get some cocoa," Dad said getting up. He pulled me to my feet. I wrapped the towel around me closer. Mom and Dad entered the cabin.

I turned and stared out into the night for a moment before going in.

Flash.

I was in the water.

A woman's scream rang out.

Fire soared through the air as pieces of debris splashed around me.

I shuddered and gasped, steadying myself on the door handle. I had thought the visions of the explosion were over. But clearly, I was wrong.

Chapter 17

We had made it back into US waters and were approaching Ketchikan. Almost like an answer to my prayers, the visions had stopped abruptly after the last one. I had finally let my guard down, and was starting to relax and enjoy the trip.

"We're going to dock here," Jim said. He pointed to a large harbor.

"Are we spending the night?" Jackson asked hopefully.

"No, just getting out to visit, and to get some exercise before we continue on. We still have a long way to travel today."

Jackson fidgeted. "When are we getting to Sitka?"

"Not for several days. Sorry it's such a long haul, but we'll be there before you know it." Jim hopped off the boat and tied it to the dock.

We got off and walked into town. Some of the buildings seemed to be propped up alongside a mountain, rising sharply into the evergreen incline. Steep wooden staircases rose from the sidewalks and ended somewhere up above us.

"This is the historical Creek Street area." Jim pointed ahead.

We approached the boardwalk and looked down at the water running underneath it.

"These shops are all built over the water," I said.

"It was too hard to blast the rock here to build anything. So, they gave up and built the walk over the creek," he said.

The shops were tiny and colorfully painted in hues of greens, blues, reds, pinks, and browns.

We walked past them, goggling at the windows full of kitschy tourist merchandise. We stopped in front of a sea foam green shop. The address said 24 Creek Street.

"What is this place?" I peered inside of one of the small-paned windows. The curtains were drawn a little, and I couldn't make out what was inside.

"Didn't you read the sign? Duh!" Jackson piped up. "It says Dolly's House."

Jim chuckled. "Dolly was a lady of the evening. This whole street here was the red light district. Business was really booming in the '20s, '30s, and '40s."

"What's a red light district?" Jackson asked.

I glanced at Mom, wondering if she'd tell Jackson.

"Uh, it's a place where ladies entertained men," Dad explained vaguely.

Jackson scrunched up his eyebrows. "Entertained men? Like, danced for them or something like that?"

"Something like that," Mom muttered.

Jackson seemed to accept this explanation. "Sounds kind of boring."

"You want to go in?" Jim asked. "It's a museum now."

"Sure." I was really curious about this Dolly person. She must have been quite a character.

We bought tickets and went inside the creaky door to the main room.

"It smells like mold in here," Jackson complained.

But I could smell more than just mildew. Slowly, the scent of strong perfume floated around my head, lilting seductively around my shoulders. Faint laughter filtered through time and tinkled through the air like wind chimes on a breeze.

"Welcome to Dolly's House!" the tour guide began. She was dressed in a red 1920s flapper dress. Her reddish brown hair was pushed aside with a black band that encircled her head. A black and red plumed feather fanned out from the back of the band as if it were waving at us.

"First, let me give you a brief history about Dolly. She was born Thelma Dolly Copeland in the state of Idaho in 1888. She moved to Ketchikan in 1919 and set up this establishment. From the 1920s through the 1940s, Creek Street was Ketchikan's red light district. All the shops you see on this boardwalk today, were at that time, brothels."

"Whoa," I muttered.

"Exactly!" The guide laughed. "That's a lot of brothels, huh? Well, this place was bustling with fishermen, miners, and loggers back then. Kind of a rough and tumble frontier town. Keep in mind that back then, prostitution was legal here, but alcohol wasn't."

Mom's eyebrows raised.

"What's prostitution?" Jackson whispered. Mom shushed him, her cheeks turning pink.

"So, to keep their gentlemen callers happy, Dolly had arranged for a special delivery. Men would row up the creek under the cloak of darkness. They paddled under the pilings until they got pretty close to where we are standing right—about here. There was a trap door under this house." She said pointing to the floor. "That's where they would hand up the alcohol, and Dolly would hand them the cash."

"Clever," Dad said.

"Indeed. Dolly was a clever and much adored favorite on Creek Street. I'll let you take a look around. Keep an eye out for the many secret doors and hiding places for stashing alcohol. There are lots of them. If you have any questions, I'll be waiting right here."

We shuffled deeper into the house. The top half of the walls were covered in floral wallpaper. A dark strip of wood topped the painted green wainscoting.

The kitchen was small. White appliances with rounded edges filled the cramped space. There was a little red table in the corner. The teapot sitting on the stove, the pots and pans, and all other dishes were all bright red, picking up the vermillion hues in the wallpaper.

We left the kitchen and wandered into Dolly's bedroom where her large brass bed stood. The silky, dusty rose bedspread was neatly made, and frilly pillows adorned the headboard.

"You are a pretty one," a woman's voice whispered in my ear. I whirled around, but no one was there. Perfume curled around my nostrils.

The rest of the group moved on without me while I tried to find the person who matched the voice.

"Jenny?" My mom came back into the room. "Aren't you coming with us?"

"I'll catch up in a bit." I pretended to look at the pictures on the wall.

"We'll be upstairs."

I could hear the group walking up the staircase, the clomping of their feet and squeaking of the stairs dissipated as they ascended.

I stepped away from the photos on the wall and looked around the room. The smell of the sweet perfume became stronger, and slowly a shape materialized a few feet in front of me.

It was Dolly.

"A beautiful girl like you would fetch a handsome price here," she said, smiling. She was wearing a light blue dress with details of lace, beads, and fringe on the

bottom hem and cuffs of the sleeves. Her brown hair was pulled up into the style of the 1920s and was finger-waved to frame her face. She appeared to be in her mid-thirties, with a curvy frame and ample bosom.

"Uh, I... I...," I stammered.

She giggled. *"Of course, we'd have to doll you up a little."*

I looked down at what I was wearing. Sweat pants, t-shirt, and hoodie. It occurred to me that I hadn't had a shower in a long time.

"I've been on a boat for a while," I answered stupidly. The very idea that I was defending my looks rather than the fact I wasn't a prostitute dawned on me.

Dolly set off into another fit of laughter.

"Oh, dearie, it's all right," she said, walking toward me. *"Here, let's go in the bathroom and see what we can do with you."*

"But I'm not..."

The lady came toward me and tried to grab my elbow. The icy cold went right through me. She frowned, and looked at my arm.

"Hmmm, yes I forgot about that," she mumbled.

Dolly glided into the bathroom, and I followed her. I stood facing the mirror and gaped—her reflection was there too.

Seeing the look on my face, she chuckled again. *"I'm a spirit, not a vampire."*

I suddenly saw the humor in the situation and let out a loud laugh.

She joined in and soon we were doubled over, holding our sides.

Finally, I straightened back up and looked in the mirror.

"Why don't you hold your hair up?" she said.

"Like this?" I asked, pulling my hair back from my face and twirling it back into a twist. I kept my hand on it to keep it from falling back down.

"Oh yes, my, my. You are a beauty," she said thoughtfully.

"Thank you."

"Your name, by any chance, wouldn't be Jenny, would it?"

My eyes widened. "How did you know that?" I gasped.

"Oh, a little bird told me," she answered. *"Anyway, you should go out onto the boardwalk. There is someone waiting to talk to you. I'll let him know that you're here."*

"What?" I turned to face her, but she had disappeared. Her perfume lingered in the air.

I went back into the bedroom and turned around slowly, looking for any sign of her. Nothing. A shiver ran up my spine.

I walked into the hall and made my way up the stairs to join our group.

Chapter 18

"I don't get why they made some dumb lady's house into a museum." Jackson rolled his eyes, looking bored.

"Personally, I thought it was very interesting," I said.

My brother sneered at me. "That's because you're boring too."

"Real mature." I quietly elbowed him as we went through the open doorway.

We stepped outside. There were tons of tourists milling about.

"Ship must be in," Jim said matter-of-factly.

"Ship?" I asked.

Jim pointed toward the water. A massive cruise ship was docked right near the harbor, dwarfing the town.

"Wow!" my mom said in surprise. "It's so big."

"All these people will make shopping here a little tricky," Jim said.

"Hey, Jackson, come here!" Dad motioned toward a shop window. "Check this out." Mom and Jim followed them to see what he'd found.

I looked around, searching for any unoccupied space. If a ghost wanted to talk to me, I was sure he or she wouldn't show themselves with so many people around. Tourists were packed twenty to thirty people deep in every direction. My eyes skipped over the horde of camera-toting sightseers. There, beyond the boardwalk, a forest of tall Douglas Fir trees edged the shops. Between two of the stores, a wooden staircase led to the timbered area. I didn't think anyone would miss me if I took off for a few moments.

I pushed through the throng of vacationers and made my way up the stairs.

At the top of the landing, a little path wove into the dense green. Sword ferns peeked out between a few stumps covered in moss. I could still hear the people on the boardwalk, but the sounds were muted.

Slowly, I turned around looking for any sign of supernatural activity. The smell of cedar, alder, and earth hung thickly in the air. A crow landed on a branch above my head and tipped his head down to meet my gaze.

Suddenly, a smoky shape began to appear several feet in front of me. I watched in fascination as it took the form of a Native American man. He was tall, and wore some sort of ceremonial robe around his shoulders. The robe was black with red trim and abalone buttons.

"*Yak'éi ixsateení,*" he said. His voice was deep and commanding.

"I'm sorry. I don't understand you." My voice shook.

He nodded. "*It is good to see you.*"

"Am I supposed to know who you are?"

"*No, but I know who you are,*" he answered. "*Jenny.*"

"What? How do you ghosts know my name?" I was astounded.

"*I am not a ghost. I am a spirit. I know that I am dead in this physical world. My soul lives on in the afterlife.*"

"Are you here all the time?" I asked.

He smiled. "*This place is too busy; too loud. I only come to visit when I find it necessary.*"

"I take it that it's necessary then."

"I am pleased to see you. I will pass on the news to the Tlingits in Sitka. They will be glad to know you are on your way."

"What do they want with me?" I asked, dumbfounded that they knew anything about me at all.

"They have been waiting for you. You are the one person who can help. Your gift is powerful. Look for the one with the raven on his side."

"But what...?"

His form dissolved into a smoky gray and dissipated into the light breeze.

I shuddered. My heart pounded faster in my chest. This was all building toward some unstoppable rollercoaster ride.

I left the wooded path and headed back to the boardwalk. It was thick with tourists. I struggled to spot my family, and then pushed through the wall of people to get to them.

"Where were you?" Mom asked. "It's hard to find anyone in this crowd."

"I had to meet with someone Dolly wanted me to see."

Mom's eyes got huge, and she pulled me by the elbow down the walkway. "You'll have to fill me in on the way back to the boat."

Chapter 19

Sitka.

The sun was shining when we puttered up to Crescent Harbor. Earlier in the morning, we had passed a myriad of tiny islands. They looked like dark green bubbles dotting the blue water. The closer we got to Sitka, the more wildlife we saw. Humpback whales, orcas, and even a fleet of dolphins racing alongside our boat, kept us oohing and aahing all morning long.

"Jenny!" Dad yelled. "Can you throw me that rope?" He had jumped off the bow onto the dock and was holding the boat in place so he could tie it to the cleat.

"Sure." I picked up the rope and threw it to him. He caught it in one swift motion. A flock of seagulls flew overhead, their calls ringing loudly in my ears.

Jim cut the engine and jumped off to help my dad tie off the other side. The boat was now expertly tethered into its slip.

I stood on the back deck and looked around. The harbor was large and housed every kind of boat imaginable. I noticed small, beat-up cabinless boats as well as a nice looking yacht several docks over.

Jackson caught my gaze and peered over to the pristine yacht. "Now that's what I'm talkin' about!" he announced. "Someday, I'm gonna have one of those babies."

"Yeah, right." I snickered.

"Am so!" he insisted. "You just wait. I'll be rich, and you can come visit me in my mansion. I might even let you swim in my pool, if you play your cards right."

"Oh, yeah? That's awfully generous of you." I rolled my eyes.

"I'm a generous kind of guy."

I shook my head and yelled down to Dad. "When can we get off the boat?"

"Have you packed up your stuff, and cleaned up?" he asked.

"Uh huh! I made sure Jackson did too."

"Great! Then, you guys can start loading all your stuff out onto the dock," he said.

Jackson and I ran in and brought out all of our stuff. We lined it all up onto the walkway.

"I had a friend bring my truck to the parking lot." Jim pulled a set of keys out of his jeans pocket. "Let's take a load up there first and then get the kitchen stuff packed up."

We spent the next half an hour going back and forth from the boat to the truck. I was exhausted by the time we had piled the last of the supplies into the vehicle.

"Good thing you have a double cab." Mom climbed into the truck, and snuggled in next to my brother. She kissed the top of his head.

"Yeah," Jackson said with a groan. "Otherwise I'd probably have to sit on Jenny's lap."

"If that were the case, I would rather walk to Jim's house," I muttered.

We rolled out of the parking lot and took a right. The stoplight was red up ahead.

"It was big news when this stoplight went in," Jim said. "I used to live here back when we didn't have any stoplights at all."

"I can't imagine driving in a town with no stoplights. There would be an endless stream of traffic accidents where we live," my dad said.

"Is this the only stoplight in town?" Jackson asked.

"No, there is another one—it's over by Swan Lake." Jim gestured up ahead.

The next stoplight appeared in front of us. We turned onto Halibut Point Road. I looked out the window at the small body of water. Lily pads floated along the edges.

Flash.

The lake was frozen.

Men were standing on the ice, sawing big hunks of it into blocks.

"That's weird," I mumbled.

"It's man-made," Jim said, almost as if he had read my mind. "The Russians dug it out. When the lake froze, they cut it up into chunks, and sold the ice to some of the communities in the Pacific Northwest."

"Enterprising," Dad commented.

The further we drove down Halibut Point Road, the more in awe I became of this place. The road skirted the water and everywhere there was the blue of the sky reflecting off the ocean. Where it wasn't blue, it was green. The trees and mountains behind bordered the water like a picture frame.

"Every house has a water view," I whispered.

"You'd pay well over a million dollars for a view like that in Seattle," Mom said.

I gazed at Sitka Sound. The volcano I had seen from the harbor appeared in the distance. A feeling of home came over me. For some reason, I felt completely at ease here.

Boom ba ba boom boom, boom ba ba boom boom.

123

"Did you hear that?"

"Hear what?" Dad asked.

"Never mind." I shook my head. The ease I felt a moment ago slipped away. It was starting again.

**

I was exhausted after unpacking my stuff in the bedroom. Luckily, the house was large enough that I didn't have to share a room with Jackson. I lay down on the twin bed, noting how soft the mattress was. The waves crashing right outside my window made my eyelids heavy and lulled me to sleep.

Flash.

I pushed the branches away from my face as I walked.

The man—Dad—wouldn't be back until tomorrow. I was alone.

How could I get off this island? Where was my mommy?

My stomach rumbled.

I remembered the hatchet left sitting by the fireplace.

If I could cut down a few small trees and tie them together, maybe I could float away from here. But I had to hide the raft where he wouldn't find it.

A huckleberry bush! We had these at home.

I plucked one off a branch and popped it into my mouth.

I woke with a start. Devon! I was so relieved he was still alive.

I pulled the cell phone out of my bag and was about to dial Detective Coalfield. I frowned and put it back down. It would be a wasted call—the vision didn't provide any more information about his location.

I got up and looked around the mostly wood-paneled room. Nothing fancy, that's for sure. The shag carpet was a

124

dull brown and looked like it was at least twenty years old. The wall that wasn't paneled with wood was painted lavender. I put my hand on the white dresser that stood along it. A vision of Jim's daughter, Callie, as a little girl popped into my head. She was in front of the gold-framed mirror, brushing her long dark hair. Her room. I smiled. It had a nice vibe.

Standing in front of the mirror, I took in my own reflection. Ack!

I grabbed my bag, dug out fresh clothes and bathroom stuff, and ran for the shower before anyone else had a chance to get there before me.

**

"Wow!" Dad said as I came out of the bathroom. "You look like your old self."

I laughed. "Thanks! I must have looked pretty bad, huh?"

"I didn't say that," he replied. "You just look a little… um… better."

I smiled and stretched. "Yeah, thanks. That was a back-handed compliment if I ever heard one."

"I'm hungry," Jackson said, sauntering into the kitchen. Mom and Dad were unpacking all of the food from the coolers.

"Take a sandwich," Mom suggested.

Jackson wrinkled his nose. "Ugh! More sandwiches? I'm sick of those."

"Too bad," Dad said. "Let's just eat these up, and then we'll go out for dessert or something."

Jim joined us in the kitchen. "I just got off the phone with Alaska Airlines. They have a seat available on the four o'clock flight."

"Leaving so soon?" Mom asked. "We just got here!"

"Well, I had planned on staying a few days, but it turns out I've got to head back to Seattle. I just checked in with my business partner, and he's having a tough time with the workload. There's a boat show coming up, and our staff is nowhere near prepared for it."

Jackson half-heartedly munched on his sandwich. "So, are we going back, too?"

"No, honey. We are staying for a few weeks." Mom ruffled his blond hair.

He took another bite.

"Why don't we all get cleaned up, and then we'll drive Jim to the airport," Dad said.

"Of course, you know that the truck is for you to drive while you are here. And help yourself to the bikes in the garage if you want to take a ride," Jim said.

"Thank you so much," Mom said. "It's so nice of you to let us stay here."

"My pleasure. I like having someone stay here. The house gets lonely when it's left alone too long."

Dad laughed. "We'll keep 'er company."

***

A few hours later, we said goodbye to Jim at the airport.

"Dad, you told us we could have dessert!" Jackson insisted.

"Jim did say there's a good place right here."

"Airport food?" I asked. "That's not my idea of a great place to eat."

"The peanut butter pie is supposed to be great," Dad said. The airport was tiny. We walked down the short hall and entered a place called The Nugget.

We all ordered the peanut butter pie. I took a bite and savored the rich, creamy texture.

"Mmmm," said Jackson.

"At least he's not talking with his mouth full this time. Peanut butter keeps his mouth glued shut."

Jackson frowned, and kicked me under the table.

"Ouch!"

Dad scowled at me. "Stop with the insults, okay? And Jackson, don't kick your sister."

"He's just been cooped up on the boat for too long," Mom said. "I've signed him up for Sitka Fine Arts Camp starting on Monday. That'll keep him busy."

"But I thought I was going to camp," I complained.

"You are, but that's the week after," Mom answered. "The middle school session is this week and then your two-week high school session starts."

"Fine Arts Camp? What?" Jackson looked horrified. "When you said you signed me up for camp, I thought you meant something fun, like soccer camp or outdoor survival camp, or something like that."

"Trust me, you'll love this," my mom said. "I've signed you up for Animation, Sculpture, Rock Band, Clowning, and Acrobatics."

"Clowning? He could teach that class himself," I muttered under my breath.

Jackson ignored me. "That sounds kind of cool."

Mom seemed relieved. "Yes, it does, doesn't it?"

"What did you sign *me* up for?" My curiosity was suddenly piqued.

"Let's see," Mom said, rummaging through her purse to find her list. "Here it is. I've signed you up for Landscape Drawing—"

"Landscape Drawing? Mom, you know how bad I am at drawing."

"Now, Jenny, I didn't want all the classes to be easy for you. Life is about rising to the occasion sometimes. Stretching beyond what you think you are capable of, right?"

"Maybe. Okay, what else?"

127

"Latin Dance, Theatre Improv, Poetry, and Musical Theatre and Cabaret Performance," she read off her list.

I took a bite of my pie while I considered her choice of classes. "They all sound pretty interesting. But I'm still worried about Landscape Drawing."

"Sounds pretty boring to me," Jackson said. He had finished his pie and was leaning back in his chair with his hands on his stomach.

"Not at all," Dad said. "I think the drawing class will be kind of relaxing for your sister. And it's a good opportunity for her to learn something new."

"Whatever," Jackson said. "I'm just glad I don't have to take the class. Sounds like torture to me."

"*You're* torture," I mumbled.

"Jenny," Mom said in warning. "I know you are sick of each other being cooped up on that boat for so long, but let's all just try to get along. By the way, you'll be staying on campus for your two-week session."

"You mean, I won't be staying with you guys?"

"I thought since you are older, you would want the full camp experience and live on campus in the dorms. It will help you bond with the rest of the campers."

"Yes!" Jackson nearly shouted, and started dancing in his seat.

Mom shook her head.

"Actually, that's okay," I agreed. "It's a bonus for me to get time away from *him*," I poked Jackson in the chest from across the table.

He slapped my hand away and stuck out his peanut-butter-coated tongue. Lovely.

* * *

The next week was sheer bliss. Jackson was gone at camp all day long. I spent my days sightseeing with Mom

128

and Dad, walking on the beach, and riding one of the bikes Jim had left in the garage.

But by the time the weekend arrived, I was feeling lonely. With a twinge of horror, I realized that I even missed bickering with Jackson. I kept sitting outside on the deck, texting Julia, Aya, and Hannah non-stop. They were anxious to know the whole scoop about Mike and how he had dumped me.

"Jerk," Julia texted.

"No," I wrote back. "Not a jerk. Just a dumb boy." My heart still ached thinking about him.

"Find yourself a hot Alaskan man," Aya texted.

"I'm done with guys," I wrote back.

"Yeah, right," Julia replied.

I added a smiley face with a wink emoji, and put my phone down on the little table next to my chair.

My mind wandered back to Mike and our time together. I was torn between longing for him and hating him for tearing us apart. Tears rolled down my cheek as I allowed myself the memory of his arms wrapped around me, pulling me close to his chest. I wiped my face, and stared out at the water. Dark, metal-gray clouds had rolled in. The water churned in angry crescendos, hard white tips on every peak. Even though it was only noon, it felt much later. The rain began in a mist at first, then increased to a solid drizzle.

I got up out of the chair, opened the sliding glass door, and entered the living room.

My phone buzzed in my hand. It was a text from Mike.

"Jenny. I miss you. Please call me." I stared at the phone for a moment. Frowning, I glanced at the screen again. My fingers hovered over the buttons. I sank onto the couch, biting my lip. I leaned over and put my head down in my hands. The phone buzzed again. My eyes got misty as I turned it off and shoved it into my pocket.

Chapter 20

Butterflies danced around in my stomach, and my hands were sweaty. It was the first day of Fine Arts Camp, and I didn't know a single soul. I tried to recall a time when I went to an event or class where I didn't know anybody. I couldn't remember even one instance. Here, no one was familiar.

"What's your first class?" A girl with dark red hair asked me. She was petite, with brown eyes and a spray of freckles on her cheeks.

"Landscape Drawing."

"Me too!" She clapped her hands. "Are you staying on campus?"

I nodded.

"Great!" Her enthusiasm was almost nauseating this early in the morning. "Which room?"

"Room 206," I said.

"OMG! That's my room number." She thrust her hand out to me. "My name is Cassandra. What's yours, roomie?"

"Jenny."

"Well, it's a pleasure to meet you, Jenny!" she said as she pumped my hand up and down. "Class doesn't start for another two hours. Let's put our stuff in our room and get set up."

"Um, okay. Is there any place we can get some black tea or maybe coffee?"

"Oh, sure! That would be in the cafeteria. We can go there after we put our stuff in the room."

My body protested as I walked up the stairs to the second floor. I hadn't gotten up early enough to eat before I left the house, and I didn't function well without food.

"Ta da!" Cassandra sang out as she flung the door open.

Oh my God. Could she be any perkier?

"Which bed do you want?"

"I don't care, you pick."

She marched over to the bunk bed, climbed the ladder, and flung herself onto it in a prone position. "Comfy!" She poked the mattress with her fingers. "Not too hard and not too soft. Yup, this will do."

Lord, God in heaven. I prayed I would make it through the morning with this chick.

Cassandra bounced up on her knees, grabbed her bag, and proceeded to unload everything onto the bed. She swiftly grabbed her clothes, jumped off without even touching the ladder, opened the dresser, and put her things away.

"See?" She extended her arms out in an exaggerated fashion. "My half on the right, and yours on the left. Does that work for you?"

I shrugged. "Sure."

She stood, waiting a moment for me to put my clothes in my half of the dresser. When I didn't make any motions to do so, she stepped forward, took the bag off my shoulder, and began emptying it.

"Whoa, whoa, whoa!" I said. "I can do that."

She gave me a knowing look. "Oh, I get it. You have something in there you don't want me to see."

"Actually, no." I was taken aback. "But I need to do it myself, or else I won't know where anything is."

"I suppose you can do this later today." She surveyed the contents of the bag.

She grabbed my arm and ushered me out the door. "Let's get breakfast before the crowd gets there. I hate it when they run out of bacon."

I shook my head. This girl was a little crazy—and I had to spend two whole weeks with her. She hurtled me down the stairs and onto the path.

"Hi, Scott! Hi Piper! Oh, hey, Josie!" Cassandra waved and smiled along the way to the cafeteria. The students waved back and continued on to their destinations.

"Guess you've come here before?" I asked as we pushed open the doors to the dining hall.

"Oh, my God, yes! This is my fifth year coming to this camp." She stopped abruptly and pointed as she talked. "Oatmeal is over there, hot food over there, baked goods over there, fruit, juice, coffee, and tea over there. I'm going straight to the bacon before it disappears. Want me to get you some?"

"No, thanks."

"Watching that figure of yours, huh? It would be tough to look like you. I bet there's a lot of pressure to keep up a body like that."

My mouth hung open, and I took a moment to regroup. "Um, not really. I like bacon, but today, I just want some oatmeal. And coffee."

She nodded, as if she knew just how I felt about oatmeal and coffee. "Meet you back at the table by the window." She marched off to get her bacon.

Compared to the cafeteria at Newport High School, this one was very small. The building itself was old, but I could tell that the wooden floors had recently been refinished and the walls freshly painted a bright white. Long tables were placed horizontally with aisles between

132

each row. There were a few small groups of campers, talking and eating.

I walked over to the oatmeal bar, grabbed a tray, and scooped some into a bowl. I added brown sugar, nuts, raisins, and a sprinkle of cinnamon. I grabbed a banana from a large metal bowl on the side of the table, and then found the beverage bar. The smell of coffee beckoned to me—even if it wasn't Starbucks. I poured myself a steaming cup of the black brew, and doctored it up with two sugar cubes and cream.

After I sat down to eat, Cassandra came back to the table and sat down across from me. She attacked the bacon on her tray with relish.

"Oh my God! This is so good! Mom and Dad never keep bacon in the house. They're health nuts."

I took a sip of my coffee. "Is this the only time you get to eat it?"

She nodded vigorously. "Except when I have a sleepover with a friend. All my friends are required to make sure their fridges are stocked with bacon before I sleep over."

My mouth involuntarily twitched into a slight smile. As obnoxious as Cassandra was, she was also entertaining.

"So, where are you from? You're obviously not from Sitka, because that's where I'm from, and I would know it if you were from here."

"Good observation." I took a bite of my oatmeal and sipped on my coffee.

"Let me guess," she said. "I don't think you are from Haines. Maybe Petersburg? I don't think you're a Ketchikan girl, and Hoonah is definitely out. Wait—it's got to be Juneau! Am I right?"

"Nope, I'm from the Seattle area."

"Seattle!" She grabbed my arm and a glop of oatmeal perched on my spoon went flying across the table and landed near a guy sitting four seats away. He gave me a funny look, and went back to his pancakes. "That is my all-time favorite city in the whole universe!"

"Have you been to all the cities in the universe?" I asked, amused.

"No, but it's the only city I've been to outside of Alaska."

"Really?"

"Yeah, but it's the best! Skyscrapers and shopping malls. No... *multiple* shopping malls!"

I laughed. "I never thought of Seattle that way."

"We go there every two years—we just get itchy to get off this island sometimes, you know?"

"I can imagine."

"That's super cool that you live there." She munched on her last piece of bacon. "So, let's compare our class schedules. Is Landscape Drawing the only one we have together?"

"I'm taking Latin Dance, Theatre Improv, Poetry, and Musical Theatre and Cabaret Performance."

Her face broke out into an even wider grin. "I'm taking Musical Theatre and Cabaret Performance too. Cool!"

"You must be a theatre kid. You are so, um... expressive," I added with a smile.

"You read me like a book." Cassandra got up from her seat. "I'm going to get some fruit and some more bacon. Want anything?"

"Sure. Maybe bacon sounds good after all." Her enthusiasm for bacon was contagious.

She winked. "I'm growing on you, aren't I?"

Chapter 21

Camp Orientation had just finished up, and Cassandra and I had run back to our room to pack up our art supplies.

"Where are we going again?" I tried catching up to my roommate, my backpack thumping up and down on my shoulder.

Her short little legs were moving in purposeful strides toward another one of the brown buildings. "Fraser Hall. It's just over there," she said, pointing at the building to the left. She pulled the door open and we both ran inside.

The door to Room 101 stood propped open. A few students sat on the floor, their backs against the wall. More campers filed in behind us. The sun streamed in through the windows, coloring the hardwood floors a rich golden hue. A large square table stood in the middle of the room. On it was placed a pot with a fern growing out of it, a piece of driftwood, and a watering can.

"Hey, guys!" said a young woman with dull brown, frizzy hair. She wore Levi cutoff shorts and a black Sitka Fine Arts Camp t-shirt. She tugged at her artsy, gold earrings. The students quieted down and gave her their attention.

"My name is Marla," she said, smiling. "If you're signed up for Landscape Drawing, you're in the right room. If not, you'd better figure out where you're going."

A couple of students laughed. One looked embarrassed and quickly scurried out.

"Why don't you grab yourself a chair," Marla said pointing to the stack in the corner. "Arrange yourselves around the table. Make sure you have your sketchpad and pencils."

Cassandra and I did as we were told and were soon sitting about four or five feet from the arrangement.

"Now, I know this is Landscape Drawing, and we'll be going outdoors soon, but first, I wanted to get a quick assessment of your drawing skills."

I groaned. Or lack thereof, I thought.

"I'm going to give you about ten to fifteen minutes to draw all or some of the elements on this table. I'll come talk to you individually when you're done and then we can move outside."

My hand holding the pencil shook while I stared at the objects on the table.

Cassandra gave me a sideways glance. "What are you waiting for?" Her whisper carried through the silent room.

This was worse than stage fright. This was drawing fright.

Marla came around to our side of the table. "Are you having trouble getting started?" she asked kindly.

"Yeah, I'm really not artistic at all." I shifted in my seat. "My mom thought it would be a good idea if I took a class outside of my comfort zone." Snickers from the other students sailed lightly through the air and ricocheted off the walls.

"No judging," Marla said to the class. "It's okay. Just really look at the shapes of what you're drawing. Don't try to draw what you think the fern *should* look like. Just draw the outlines and shapes of what you see. It takes the pressure off."

I nodded and bent over my sketchbook. Ten minutes later when Marla called time, I looked down at what I had drawn. A demented-looking fern and a watering can that looked like Mrs. Pots from Disney's *Beauty and the Beast*. I glanced at Cassandra's drawing and was astonished to see an image that looked like it was created by an Italian master from the Renaissance period.

"Jesus, Cassandra," I said under my breath. "That's gorgeous."

"This?" She shrugged. "It's not my best work. I obviously rushed it. Let's see yours." She tugged my sketchbook over to her lap. Marla stood over her shoulder, looking at my drawing. Cassandra's eyes widened.

"You weren't kidding when you said you didn't have any drawing experience, were you?" Cassandra asked.

Marla held up my sketchbook and examined the drawing. "Well, it's a start. Actually, you've done a nice job bringing some life into your drawing. I like how the watering can has almost human characteristics."

I felt the color blossoming in my face. Oh, God.

"I didn't mean to embarrass you. What's your name?"

"Jenny," I mumbled.

"I'm sorry, Jenny." She chuckled. "I really didn't intend to make you feel bad. Your drawing may not be super realistic, but it has other qualities that make it really interesting. I think you're going to enjoy this class and get a lot out of it."

Ugh. I wanted to kick my mom for signing me up for this.

"Okay, everyone, stand up," Marla announced. "We are pairing up and heading to Totem Park to draw. Like I said before, pay attention to the shapes, not the objects themselves. And negative space is just as important as the positive space."

Several of the campers looked at her with puzzled expressions.

"I guess I should define that." Marla ran her fingers through her hair. "So, positive space is the actual object you are looking at." She pointed at a chair. "And negative space is the air around the object, which actually has a shape as well." Her fingers traced the area between the chair legs, showing the negative space trapped within the wooden supports. "Does that make sense?"

Nodding, I smiled at Cassandra and put my backpack on my shoulder. For once, I actually understood an artistic term.

"Where do you want to go draw?" Cassandra asked me.

"Nope," Marla said, separating us. "Don't pair up with someone you know. I'd like you to find a new person to pair up with. We'll get to know each other faster this way—it's kind of like an icebreaker."

I glanced around the room. I wasn't sure I was ready for this.

Cassandra spied a skinny blond boy that looked like he weighed ninety pounds soaking wet, and dashed over to him.

"Hi!" She thrust her hand out to shake his. "My name is Cassandra! What's your name, and where are you from?"

The boy looked stunned and mumbled something.

"Well, nice to meet you, Kevin from Ketchikan." She threw her head back and laughed. "Kevin from Ketchikan! I like that." She linked her arm through his and tugged him out the door.

I grinned and shook my head.

"Dude. Over there. Go get 'er, tiger," someone said and shoved a dark-haired boy at me. The shover laughed as the guy he pushed nearly knocked me over.

"Jerry—cut it out!" he said angrily. "Sorry about that."

I regained my balance. "It's okay. You couldn't help it."

"I'm Tyler," he said. "Ty for short. Who are you?"

"I'm Jenny."

We left the room and walked outside.

"Do you know where you're going?" I asked.

"Yeah, I live here." He headed toward the road. "Just follow me."

About ten minutes later, we had arrived in Totem Park. We'd walked in silence. This guy wasn't much of a talker, that much was clear.

"Where should we sit?" I asked, hoping that would get the conversation started a little.

He pointed toward a path near the water. "Let's go over there. We can sit on the beach and draw." His face was a mask of indifference; I couldn't get a good read on him. Did he even have a personality?

I hurried after him. When we got to the beach, he hopped nimbly from rock to rock, and sat down on a big log. It was smooth with age and weathered to a bone white. I climbed clumsily on to the log and sat down a few feet away from him. He scooted a little further away.

Wow. Maybe he didn't like girls. Or, maybe he didn't like me.

"So, you live here?" I tried again to break the silence.

"That's what I said, isn't it?"

"Uh, yeah. Okay—how long have you lived here?" I opened up my backpack and got out my sketchbook and pencil.

He was already drawing, staring out at the water. "My whole life."

"You're lucky," I said. "It's a beautiful place." I took a moment to study his profile. He was handsome. His dark hair swept over his eyes and he brushed it away. The black lashes fringed his chocolate brown eyes. They held a certain sadness to them. I wondered what would make a guy his age so sad.

I looked out at the water and tried to pick a subject to draw. Behind the harbor to the right, the volcano loomed. I

139

thought if I had even an ounce of artistic skill, I could draw that. Instead, I tried something simpler. There were a few small islands in the distance, so I focused on drawing their shapes and the water around them. I fell into a zen-like mode and actually enjoyed the process. I had forgotten that Ty was even there until he looked at his watch.

"We better head back," he said.

"Already? That was fast."

"I guess." He got up.

I closed my sketchbook, threw it in the backpack, and slung it over my shoulder. I stood up on the log and then jumped down, twisting my ankle as I landed on some rocks and driftwood. I winced and went down on one knee.

Suddenly, he was beside me, putting a protective arm around my shoulders. "Are you all right?"

I couldn't figure out what startled me the most... the fact that I had twisted my ankle or that he was actually being nice to me.

"Yeah, I'm okay," I tried to stand up, but my ankle gave out, and I sucked in a quick gasp of air.

"No, you're not. Here let me help you." In one quick motion, he put one arm under my knees and the other under my back and scooped me up. He set me lightly onto a rock and crouched down by my injured ankle.

I stared at him. Was this the same guy who could barely grunt out a word or two when I asked him a question? And damn! He was strong. He had lifted and carried me as if I were no heavier than a feather.

"Let's see what we've got here." He examined my ankle. "It doesn't look too bad—yet. But it could start swelling if we don't get some ice on it soon."

"Ice," I repeated. "I don't think there is any ice around here."

"Just a sec." He got up and ran down the beach toward the water. In less than a minute, he came back carrying a clump of wet seaweed.

"Take your sock and shoe off," he ordered.

I untied my Converse shoe and slipped off my sock. Ty took the dripping seaweed and wrapped it around my ankle—my leg jerked with the shock of the cold water. My face wrinkled up in disgust.

"I know it's kind of gross, but let's just hold it here for a minute or so. It works wonders, I promise." His dark hair fell over his eyes again and he brushed it away with one hand while still holding the seaweed to my ankle with the other.

"If you say so." I wasn't sure what else to say to him. It was an awkward moment.

Finally, he removed the seaweed and used the bottom of his t-shirt to dry my ankle.

"Okay, you can put your sock and shoe back on." He got up from his crouch and wiped the sand off his jeans.

I quickly pulled my sock and shoe on and tied the laces.

He held his hand out to me. "Test your weight on it."

I stood up and shifted my body a little. "Hey! It feels good. It doesn't hurt at all. How did you do that?"

He shrugged. "Don't know. Just something my grandparents taught me."

"Well, they are wise people." I took a few steps forward. My ankle felt perfectly normal.

"Let's get going," he said abruptly. "We'll be late getting back to class."

We booked it back to the classroom and were the last ones through the door. However, everyone was still chatting, so we weren't in trouble. The instructor had moved the still life items and the table to the back of the room. She stood inside the circle of chairs.

"Sorry I didn't get a chance to check in with each of you at Totem Park. So, if I haven't looked at your work yet, come on up here and let me take a look at your drawings—I'm anxious to see your compositions.

Tomorrow, we'll talk more about how to compose an interesting drawing with perspective, and using contrast to make your work come to life. Grab your chairs and put them in a stack in the corner on your way out. Thanks, and see you tomorrow!"

About half of the class packed up their stuff, put their chairs away, and left the room. There were about three pairs of students left, including Ty and me, Cassandra and Kevin from Ketchikan, and two girls whom I didn't know.

Marla looked at Kevin and Cassandra's work. Cassandra, of course, monopolized the conversation good-naturedly.

"Bravo!" Marla announced after checking their art. "You are both very talented. Cassandra, I love your use of shading—very dramatic. Kevin, I'm impressed with the level of detail you've achieved in such a short amount of time. Nice work!"

I cringed as I realized that Ty and I were next.

"Let's see, Ty," Marla said. She held up his drawing. "Oh, this is nice. This is almost painterly, what you've done here. And you've captured the harbor and Mt. Edgecumbe so well in just a few strokes. Really good."

My breath caught in my chest as she approached me.

"Jenny—let's see yours," Marla said. I handed her the sketchbook and she flipped it open. She gasped. I closed my eyes, dreading her assessment. "*You* drew this?" She looked confused.

I nodded glumly. She hated it, I just knew it.

"My God! This doesn't look anything like the drawing you did in class. The style is entirely different. I'm at a loss for words." She held the sketchbook open for me to see.

My heart stopped. Instead of the islands I thought I had drawn, a sketch of an entirely different island appeared on the page. It was better than anything I had ever drawn in my life. The vantage point was from the water, looking straight onto a large island. The water lapped against the rocks and shore. The trees were shaded with heavy strokes, making them look like they could be moving with the wind.

Ty looked at me, his brows furrowing together in the middle.

"That's so weird." I scratched my head. "I don't remember drawing anything like that. I thought I was drawing a couple of islands in the distance."

"Are you sure you drew this?" Marla asked suspiciously, her head cocked to the side.

"No, I'm not sure." I was dazed. "That's the sketchbook I brought to class, and that's what I drew in at the beach. But…"

"Ty?" Marla looked at him. "Can you explain this?"

Ty wiped his face blank of expression. "I saw her drawing, and that's the same sketchbook."

"You didn't draw this for her?" Marla asked.

"How would I have time to draw my own sketch and then do hers? I swear—she drew that on her own."

"Huh," Marla said. "Well, that is the single greatest improvement I have ever seen in my life. I just don't get it. But, if you have drawn this, Jenny, then I say, great job. I'm completely in awe of it."

I swallowed hard. What was going on?

"Marla, I honestly don't know what to tell you," I answered slowly. "The only thing I can think of is that I kind of had a zen-like feeling when I was drawing. It was like I wasn't even aware of my surroundings."

She nodded, closed my sketchbook, and handed it back to me. "I think it's great that you were able to let go and draw like that. I'm really looking forward to seeing what you do in class tomorrow."

"Me too." I laughed nervously. "I have no idea what will be on that page next time."

Cassandra was waiting in the hall. "Ready for the next class?" she asked.

"I'm not sure," I whispered. Ty walked past me. He had the oddest look on his face—a look that was something between horror and awe.

"Bye, Ty!" Cassandra called out to him. "Ha! Bye, Ty!" She giggled profusely and then shook her head. "First there's Kevin from Ketchikan and now Bye, Ty! I'm lovin' this morning!"

Chapter 22

Clouds had moved in from the west and it was getting a little chilly. I dug into my backpack and took out my hoodie. My mind wandered back to the picture I'd drawn during Landscape Drawing, and the look on Ty's face when the class was over. What did he think of me?

I pulled my hoodie on and slung my pack onto my shoulder. My phone buzzed in my pocket. A text from Benny, back in Seattle. It read, "Guess who took me fishing today?"

"Frank?" I texted back.

"Yeah! What are you doing?"

"Can't talk. On way to class. Catch you later."

"Ok."

"Hi, Jenny!" Cassandra said. We met on the path to Allen Auditorium where the Musical Theatre and Cabaret Performance class was held.

I smiled back at her. "I wonder what material we'll be working on in this class."

"That's the best part," she said. "We get to write our own show!"

"Really? Do we know how to do that?"

"Not yet, but we will. I think we're mostly adapting existing material, but maybe we'll get to write a story around the songs," she said.

We rounded the corner and entered through the doors. My phone buzzed again. It was Mike. "I miss you," it read. Why did he keep texting me? He'd dumped me. Unless, he'd had a change of heart.

Cassandra grabbed the phone away and looked at the screen. "Who's Mike?"

I snatched my phone back and put it in my pocket. "Nobody."

"Well, 'Nobody' misses you." She giggled. "An old flame?"

"I guess."

"You'll have to tell me more about this 'Nobody' later." She grinned at me.

***

After lunch, we walked to our next class. A group of students were outside, working on carving a big totem pole. The log was horizontal and elevated on wooden supports. The campers were each carving a section of the pole.

We walked around them, looking interestedly at their progress.

"There's Ty," Cassandra whispered. I had already noticed him before she pointed him out. He bent over the design, carving away a section, his biceps bulging with the strain of the work. A trickle of sweat ran down the side of his face.

"Damn, he's hot!" She admired him as we passed by.

"Shhh! He'll hear you."

"So?"

"So—he'll think I like him, and it will inflate his ego."

"What do you care?" she asked innocently. "You already have a 'Nobody' in your life. Wait. Are you interested in Ty?"

"No," I said, too quickly. "It's just that I don't want him to think that I like him. I have two weeks of class with him, and it would be awkward if he thought that."

"Oh, shoot!" Cassandra shouted. "We're late. See you soon!" She zoomed off on the path to the left.

I stood shaking my head, watching her run. She was quite fast for such a shorty. I got out my map and surveyed the campus. My Poetry class was in the building right in front of me, so luckily I didn't have to bust a gut getting there. I glanced over my shoulder and took one last look at Ty, working on his carving.

***

"Writing poetry is a time for reflection," Branson, our teacher, said. We sat on the floor with our notebooks and pencils sprawled in front of us. "It's a time to look inward and search for deeper meaning."

I shifted uncomfortably and freed my left leg, which had been pinned underneath me. It was starting to fall asleep, and the needle-like prickles took my attention away from the instructor for a moment. He described different poem structures and read several examples out loud to us. My other leg fell asleep, and I shifted it to a different position.

Branson walked over to the window and peered out. "Ah—the clouds have gone. Perfect. Grab your stuff and go outside. I want you to find a quiet place where you can write something profound."

The students laughed.

"Just kidding." He smiled. He was young—maybe in his early twenties, but already he had a prudent, professorial way about him. At first glance, he could have been mistaken for a camper. His tousled dark hair, day-old stubble, and crumpled clothing made him look like he had just rolled out of bed.

"Does it have to rhyme?" the girl next to me asked.

"No," he answered. "Just write what comes naturally to you. It doesn't have to be in any particular style. Tomorrow, we'll try writing several different styles, but today, I just want you to write whatever is in here," he said, patting his chest.

We got up off the floor and shuffled out of the building. The campers scattered in different directions, seeking a private place to write. I wandered over to an empty bench and sat down. Branson was right. The sun was out. I raised my face and closed my eyes, letting it penetrate and warm my skin. What would I write about? Nothing popped into my head. Not a thing.

I didn't know how much time had passed, but I knew that I needed to get something on paper quickly. Maybe if I looked around, I could find some inspiration. I opened my eyes and let out a yelp. A raven sat on the other end of the bench, its shrewd black eyes surveying me.

"Caw!" It opened its wings and leapt into the air. I watched it sail over the trees. I shivered. That was weird. But now, I had an idea for a poem. I opened the notebook on my lap and began to write.

On the wings of a raven,
I bid you farewell,
My friend I adored,
And loved you so well,
We will meet again soon,
In the golden light,
I won't rest well,
'Til you're in sight.

A breeze blew over me and ruffled the pages of my notebook. I looked up just as Branson came toward the bench.

"I'm trying to get everyone to head back to the classroom. Are you finished writing?" He plunked down on the bench beside me.

"Yeah, I think so."

"May I read it?"

"Sure." I handed him the notebook. He read the poem silently.

"It's beautiful. And a little sad." He gave me a curious look. "Are you writing about your own personal experience?"

"I don't know."

"Perhaps about someone you didn't have a chance to say goodbye to?"

Was it about Mike? "I'm not sure what I was writing about. The words just came to me. Weird, huh?"

He laughed. "No, not weird. Sometimes writing is like therapy. The Muse takes us by the hand and leads us to the darkest parts of our hearts so we can heal. Writing about it releases those feelings that sometimes we never knew we had."

I nodded slowly. Maybe this *was* about Mike.

"Come on." He got up from the bench. "Help me find all the students and get them back to class."

Chapter 23

Walking into Allen Auditorium for the second time that day, I surveyed the group of campers talking animatedly and laughing. There were about eight girls and six boys. I scanned their faces, looking for any familiar students from my other classes.

The dance teacher zipped into the center of the room and clapped her hands together. She was a beautiful Latina lady in her mid-thirties, with dark ringlets bouncing on her mocha shoulders. She swept her hair into a ponytail as she talked.

"Welcome to Latin Dance!" Her red and black salsa skirt swished around her toned legs as she walked briskly to the stage. "How many of you have ever taken a dance class?"

Several of the girls raised their hands. The boys stood there, smirking.

"No? You boys there?" She pointed to the group of them. They shook their heads. Suddenly, I recognized one of them. It was Ty. Strange—he didn't seem like the type of guy who would take a dance class. He looked vaguely uncomfortable, shifting his weight from one leg to the other.

"Let me ask you a few more questions. How many of you took this class because the other classes you wanted to take were full?"

Ty and one other boy raised their hands. Some of the girls rolled their eyes.

"How many of you took this class because it was an excuse to hit on girls?" she asked with a grin.

Silence hung in the air for a brief moment, and then the rest of the guys raised their hands. The room erupted into laughter.

"I thought so," the instructor said. "Oh! My goodness, I almost forgot to tell you who I am. My name is Aurelia La Cruz. I'm originally from Venezuela, and I am a classically-trained ballet dancer."

The students looked confused. Some of the guys looked scared.

Aurelia laughed. "Don't worry. I won't be teaching you ballet. You see, I'm also trained in Latin dance."

Breathing sighs of relief, the boys' faces relaxed, and they started elbowing each other. A tall skinny guy with a broad smile did a makeshift pirouette and promptly fell on his butt. The room roared again.

"Ah, I see that you *do* need some ballet training," she said to the boy.

His smile quickly vanished. The other boys pulled him back up, grins plastered on their faces.

"So, let's get started. First, I'll teach you some basic steps, and then we can partner up and see if we can practice as couples."

The steps she taught us were basic and easy for me to pick up. Many of the boys were struggling and looking completely ridiculous as they tripped over their own feet.

Finally Aurelia stopped us. "Let's try this with partners." She began pairing us up according to height. "Here," she said grabbing Ty by the arm and pushing him toward me. "You two make a very nice couple. You are proportioned well to match one another."

My heart did a little thump in my chest. Ty made me a little nervous. I couldn't tell if I was attracted to him or kind of scared of him. Suddenly, Mike's face popped into my head, and I felt instantly guilty for even wondering if I was attracted to another boy. A thread of anger wove itself through my heart. Why should I feel guilty? Mike dumped me. I stepped toward Ty and smiled. His face was blank—unreadable, but I thought I detected a hint of a blush in his cheeks.

"You two girls," Aurelia said, pointing at a couple of students. "We don't have enough boys to go around—you'll have to be dance partners." The girls looked relieved. They were younger, probably ninth graders. I remembered how awkward I felt around boys at that age. It seemed like forever ago.

"Okay, dancers!" the instructor shouted. "Latin dance is very sensual."

Nervous giggles resounded in the auditorium.

"So, even if you feel nothing for the person you are dancing with, you fake it. Pretend that you are dancing with the sexiest person alive!"

More laughter.

"Except you two girls," Aurelia said. "I don't want you to feel awkward. But if you have some acting skills, why not ham it up and have fun with it?"

The girls burst out laughing and took their cue from the teacher, holding hands and giving each other fake smoldering looks.

"Can we watch?" one of the guys asked.

"Oh, you naughty boy!" the teacher smiled. "No, no, let's focus on the dancing." She walked to the boom box on the side of the stage and turned on the music. "Face your partners!" she yelled.

Ty and I faced each other. He was about five-foot-ten. Not as tall as Mike for sure, but Aurelia was right. Height-wise, he was a perfect dance partner for me.

"Now hold each other's hands!" she shouted.

Ty stood there, momentarily stunned. I waited a moment and then reached out to grab his hands.

Flash.

Ty stood facing the girl with the long dark hair.

"You are too funny, mister," she said with a smile in her eyes.

"What?" he answered. "You don't believe me?"

"Of course not. You did not see Sasquatch back there!" She swatted him playfully. "You tried that on me when we were kids, and it didn't work then. Why would you think it would work now?"

Ty's face broke into a wide grin. "Guess I can't fool you, huh?"

The vision dissolved.

"Come on," Aurelia said as she put her hands on her hips. "You need to swing back and forth like this!"

I shuddered a little and moved with the music. Ty looked confused and began dancing with the rhythm. Who was that girl in the vision? His girlfriend?

***

After dinner, Cassandra and I were lying in our bunks. She was reading a fantasy novel and was completely immersed in it.

My phone buzzed.

"What's up?" Benny texted.

"Just relaxing. And you?" I texted back.

"Frank's been getting vibes on that lost boy."

"What?" I texted, suddenly sitting up and bonking my head on the bunk above.

"He's on an island," he responded.

153

"Yeah, I know."

"Somewhere near Sitka."

"Uh huh, I got that too. Do you know exactly where?"

"No. Frank's working on it."

"Ok," I texted. "Let me know if he sees anything else."

"Will do," Benny replied. "Over and out."

"Roger," I texted, smiling. Whoa… this was an interesting turn of events. Frank was picking up on Devon too. What did that mean? Maybe if I focused on Devon right now, I could see him. I closed my eyes and pictured the boy in my mind. I took a deep breath and silently asked God, my angels, and spirit guides to help me. Nothing. Ugh.

My phone rang.

"Yeah, Benny, anything else?" I asked.

"Uh… who is Benny?" a voice said on the line.

"Mike?" I stammered.

"Jenny, I need to talk to you," he said. "It's so good to hear your voice."

Silence.

"Jenny?"

"Yeah. Why are you calling me?"

"I wanted to apologize. I'm so sorry—I can't stand this. I mean, I don't want to lose you."

Carefully, I changed position on my bed, hunkering down against the wall with my knees up. I grabbed my pillow and put it between my chest and my legs and hugged it tightly. My palms started to sweat, and my heart raced at a full gallop.

"Are… are you saying that you want to get back together?" I bit my lip.

"Yes. I mean, no. I mean… I don't know what I mean. I care about you—a lot. Life without you is so empty. Can we be friends and keep communicating? I miss you so much."

"Wait, I don't understand," I said. "So, you don't want to get back together, but you want to remain friends so we can... talk?"

"Yes. I mean, no. Ugh! I mean, I'd love it if we could keep up our friendship. But I think for my first year at college, we should keep it light. You know... not serious."

Anger welled up inside me. "Really, Mike? Guess what? After your freshman year, I'll be a freshman. You will have gone an entire year without any 'distractions.' And if I want to do well in my first year of college, maybe I shouldn't let *you* be a distraction! How about your junior year? Will I be a distraction then? And don't forget about when you graduate and get your first job. We should probably just break up again then, so you can concentrate on your career!"

"Jenny, wait! I—"

I hung up.

Cassandra's head appeared upside down over the edge of the top bunk. Her auburn curls bounced lightly.

"What was that all about? Was that Nobody? Did he break up with you?"

I shook my head glumly. "No, he already broke up with me. He said he misses me and wants to keep being friends."

"Friends?" Cassandra practically shouted. "Sounds to me like he wants to have his cake and eat it too."

I wiped the tears from my cheeks. Mike had no right to call me here—to ruin my perfectly nice camp experience. Sadness and hurt rumbled in my chest. My body felt hot and sweaty.

Climbing out of the bed, I grabbed my hoodie and turned to Cassandra, who was sitting on the edge of her bunk with her short legs dangling.

"I need to go for a walk," I announced.

"Do you want some company?"

155

"No, thanks. I just need to be alone right now." I opened the door.

"Be back by ten o'clock. Curfew, you know!"

I nodded and closed the door behind me.

Walking briskly down the path, I shivered slightly as the breeze picked up, cooling the perspiration on my skin. I pulled my hoodie on and made my way to the road that led to Totem Park.

When I got there, I picked a path in the forest and let my feet go. Tears streamed down my face and my stomach churned. How could he do this to me? The mixed signals he kept sending...

Although it was still light outside, and would be until past curfew, it was dimmer under the canopy of Douglas Fir and Sitka Spruce trees. I followed the path, feeling a little better as my feet led the way. The earthy smell arose from the path, and all around me the bushes and ferns gave off a pleasant green scent. A side path caught my eye, and I ambled onto the narrow trail. In just a few yards, it opened up and suddenly I was standing on the edge of the beach. The tide was high, but there was plenty of beach grass, logs, and rocks ahead before the water hit the shore's edge.

Looking out onto the iron-gray water, the wind was briny and tickled my face when a gust brought an occasional spray of salt. I hugged myself tightly—it was chillier than earlier today.

Mike. Why couldn't I get him out of my head?

I turned my gaze toward the ocean again. A small boat bobbed along, fishing poles stretched out, reaching toward the water.

Flash.

A large wooden ship was anchored not far from the shore. Two smaller ships flanked its side.

Cannon fire burst from the big ship. A cannonball whooshed past my head and smacked into a thick log fortress behind me. I whipped around, nearly jumping out of my skin with the sounds of battle all around.

Crouching behind a big driftwood log, I watched with horror as Indians fought with axes, knives, and even firearms. Men further down the shore were fighting the Tlingits. They were dressed in European clothing. Screams of pain and rage rang through the air, mixed with the sound of crashing waves.

My heart banged in my chest as I heard a high shriek echo past. I looked in time to see a muscular man, clothed in a red and black tribal garment, run full throttle toward the group of European men. I couldn't see his face—it was covered with a mask. The top of it was carved like the head of a raven. He was carrying a short, axe-like weapon. His arm flung back and then forward as he threw the axe. It soared over my head and embedded itself with a thwack into the chest of a man wearing a dark gray colonial-looking suit. The man's eyes went blank, his face slackened and he dropped to his knees. He fell, face-first, onto the rock-strewn beach.

A scream escaped my lips, and I fell sideways onto the log I was crouched behind.

"Jenny?" A hand reached out and touched my shoulder.

My eyes flew open in shock.

"Are you all right?" It was Ty.

I was shaking so badly, my legs could not unlock from my squatting position. He put his hands under my arms and gently pulled me up.

He led me over to a nearby rock and helped me sit down.

I looked into his warm, brown eyes. "How? Why... are you here?" I was still trembling and breathing hard.

Ty looked down at his feet. "Actually, I was just coming out of the cafeteria, and I noticed you leaving campus. You looked upset, so I followed you. What happened?" He looked concerned.

My bitter laugh was lost in the wind. "If I told you, Ty, you'd think I was crazy."

"Try me," he said.

My breathing was still rapid and shallow. He put his hand on my back. Heat radiated from his fingers and spread from my back to my chest. The adrenaline that had been zipping through my body subsided. I took a deep breath.

"Are you sure you want to know?"

He nodded. "I'm sure."

I carefully began to tell him about my psychic abilities, all the while trying to read his face. Could I trust him? He didn't look freaked out. When I told him about the battle I had just witnessed, his eyebrows rose.

He remained quiet for some time. He reached his hand out to me, and I took it, puzzled as to what he was thinking. Ty pulled me up to a standing position. "Come on," he said. "I want to show you something."

What was he thinking? Was he going to pretend that I never told him any of this?

Silently, we walked back down the path, toward the Visitor's Center. It was already nine o'clock, and the hours on the door said it closed at five. Ty took a key from his pocket and unlocked the door.

"My uncle works here," he said with a shrug. "I come after hours to help him carve totem poles and stuff." He held the door open for me, and I entered the building. The doors shut behind us. Inside, the lobby area was quiet. Large display cases containing Tlingit blankets, ceremonial robes, and bentwood boxes lined the walls. A janitor squirted cleaner on the glass cases and was wiping away fingerprints and smudges. He nodded to us as we passed through.

"Is the movie still running, Gus?" Ty asked him.

He nodded. "I haven't had a chance to clean the theatre yet. Go on in."

We walked through a large open room lined with more display cases and short, squat totem poles. On the other side of the room, the door to a small theatre was propped open.

We slipped into the dark room and sat down in the back row. The film was just ending and the credits were rolling. The screen went black, and the film started up again. I sat, mesmerized, as the narrator told of the history of Sitka and the invasion of the Russians in the late 1700s and early 1800s. I gasped as black and white drawings of the battle I had just witnessed on the beach played out on the screen.

The film ended, and we got up and left the theatre.

"Well," Ty said quietly. "What do you think of that?"

I blew out a breath. "Weird. Fascinating. Disturbing."

"You definitely have some sort of gift," he remarked.

I chewed on my lip. "Can we get out of here?"

"Sure."

Our footsteps echoed through the room as we walked across the wood floor. The double doors closed quietly behind us.

***

On the way back, my mind raced. What was Ty thinking? Wouldn't he have questions? Why wasn't he saying anything?

My feet came to a halt. He stopped and looked back at me. "What?" he said.

"Aren't we going to talk about this?"

"What do you want to talk about?"

My eyebrows shot up. "Oh, come on. I just told you that I witnessed a full-on battle at the beach. I told you that

I'm psychic… and you don't think we have anything to talk about?"

"Oh. *That.*"

I shook my head. "Yeah, that. You've got to be wondering if I'm crazy. I mean, maybe you're thinking, 'Wow, this chick is completely nuts. She's off her rocker.' Right?"

A slight smile tugged at the corners of his mouth. His cheeks dimpled. "Actually, I don't think you're crazy at all. You're definitely *interesting*, but not crazy."

My jaw dropped.

Ty laughed. "Okay, okay. It's just that my grandfather is a shaman. He told me you were coming. I guess I was expecting you."

All the air escaped from my lungs. The sound of the ocean, and the birds that I heard singing just a few moments ago stopped. I felt dizzy. "You were expecting me?" I whispered.

He nodded his head slowly. "But what I didn't expect is that you would be so pretty."

***

After we arrived back on campus, I went back to my room. Cassandra was sleeping with her iPod plugged into her ears, her book lying open on her stomach. A little trickle of drool escaped the corner of her mouth.

I tiptoed over to my bunk, and quickly undressed. I pulled on a pair of sweats and a t-shirt and climbed in, trying not to clunk my head on the overhead rail.

Staring at the support boards on the mattress above me, I waited for sleep to come. No such luck. Thoughts assaulted me from every angle. Mike. Ty. The visions of Russians cutting up ice on Swan Lake, and then the battle between them and the Tlingits. Why was I seeing that? It had nothing to do with Devon. And nothing to do with the

160

visions of a boat exploding. If I was going to keep getting random visions about history, I would probably go crazy. What was next...visions about George Washington or Abraham Lincoln?

When I had arrived in Sitka, I had felt an increase in energy; that much was certain. It was as if my psychic antennae had just converted to a supernatural satellite dish and was picking up every echo of the past. Was there something about this place that caused this? Or was it because my abilities were developing more rapidly than ever before?

No matter how many questions I had asked Ty, he wouldn't fully explain about his grandfather. He was expecting me? How could that be? He didn't even know me. I thought back to the spirit I had talked to in Ketchikan. He had said, *"I will pass on the news to the Tlingits in Sitka. They will be glad to know you are on your way."*

It still didn't make any sense to me. Groaning, I rolled over to my side.

Finally, as my eyelids became heavy, images of Ty's liquid brown eyes, and his warm hands touching my back, lulled me into slumber. Right before I entered a deeper state of sleep, Ty's face morphed, blurring so I could hardly make out his features. Green eyes came into focus as the boy's features dissolved, and Mike's face appeared in place of Ty's.

Sneaking through the trees, my foot came down on a twig, snapping it. I looked over my shoulder, hoping that the man wasn't back yet.

Finally, I made it to my hiding place. I uncovered the thin logs I had cut with the hatchet I'd found by the fireplace. Just a few more to go, and I could start tying them together.

Would the raft sink or float?

I looked at the blisters on the palms of my small hands. Would I be able to cut just two or three more?

Chapter 24

"Today, we'll be doing some nature drawings, but instead of landscapes, we'll be focusing on close-ups. You can draw flowers, rocks, or whatever you like," Marla said. "Let's all walk to Totem Park together." She motioned for us to gather our things.

Cassandra popped up from her seated position and flung her pack onto her back. "Come on, Jenny!" She turned to look at the boy behind her. "Kevin from Ketchikan, you are welcome to join us."

Kevin smiled haltingly, and looked around the room to see if anyone would come to his rescue. When no one did, he turned his attention back to us. "Yeah, uh, sure," he said.

Ty appeared at Kevin's side. "Mind if I come along?"

"The more, the merrier," Cassandra crooned. She linked arms with Kevin and Ty and hustled them out of the room. I half expected her to sing, "We're off to see the wizard."

When we got to the park, we took a path skirting the beach.

"I know where some Sitka roses are," Ty said. "Those might be nice to draw."

"Oooh! I love Sitka roses!" Cassandra exclaimed. "They smell so good!"

Sure enough, a hedge of roses lined a walkway up ahead. We climbed over a log on the beach and sat facing the roses. Kevin turned around and began drawing driftwood instead.

"I see a clump of seaweed over there," Ty announced. "I think I'll try drawing that."

"Guess it's just you and me then," Cassandra said with a wink.

I flipped my sketchbook cover open and took out a pencil. The bees hummed pleasantly around the magenta-colored flowers. My pencil skated across the paper as I began to sketch. Soon after I began drawing, I was lost in the perfume of the hedge roses and the tangy brine of the ocean.

"Can I see that?"

I jumped. "Oh! You startled me!"

Ty's face peered down at my sketchbook, his expression was very serious.

"Uh, sure," I said, handing it to him.

He took the sketchbook and gasped.

God, what did I draw this time?

"It's... her," he breathed. He sat down on a log. Staring at the drawing, his face contorted with emotion.

What the—? What was he talking about?

On the page of my sketchbook, was the face of a girl. She was lying on her side, her long dark hair curving with the arc of her cheek. Her eyes were closed, as if she were sleeping. It was the girl I had fleetingly seen in my vision—when I had first touched Ty's hands in our dance class.

Ty wiped the tear from his face. "It's happening... just like Grandfather said it would. You know where she is, don't you? Tell me where she is!"

"What? I don't understand."

I turned to look at Cassandra, hoping that she would help me understand. Her eyes were as round as saucers.

"It's River," she gasped. "Ty's cousin."

"Ty's cousin?" I whispered.

Cassandra nodded. "She… uh, there was an accident. A couple of months ago."

Ty's shoulders shook. His hands covered his face.

I glanced at Cassandra and then knelt down beside him. "Are you all right?"

"No."

"Is your cousin okay?" I asked.

He didn't answer. I looked up at Cassandra, whose face had gone pale. "Cassandra? What's going on?"

She looked down. "Like I said, there was an accident. It was a boat accident. River and her mom were never found."

Boat accident? Suddenly, my psychic antennae vibrated with an intensity that I had never felt before.

Flash.

I was on a boat, rocking gently on a dark ocean—the sky black, except for the luminescent moon. I was mesmerized by the light dancing on the glistening water.

A sharp pain in my head caught me off balance, and I toppled headlong into the salty spray. Orange light shone through my closed eyelids as I heard another woman's screams.

My eyes flew open in horror. Oh my God. This was it. This was the vision I had been having over, and over, and over. It wasn't about Mike on his trip. It wasn't about me on my boat trip, and it wasn't even about Devon. It was about River. I grabbed Ty's arm. His hands came away from his face, and he looked at me.

"What is it?" he gasped. "What do you know about this?"

Cassandra knelt down alongside me. "Excuse me," she said politely. "I have no idea what is going on here. Why would Jenny know anything about River? She wasn't even here when the accident happened."

165

I turned to her, wanting to get this part over with so I could explain my visions to Ty. "I'm psychic."

She snorted. "Yeah, right! Jenny, cut it out. This is serious. Can't you see that Ty's upset? He and River were inseparable."

"She's serious, Cassandra," Ty whispered. "She really is psychic."

Cassandra's eyebrows shot upwards. "Are you guys messing with me? 'Cause it's not funny."

I shook my head. "This is for real."

For once, she was speechless.

"Okay, let me explain something," I said.

I told them about all the visions I had been having this summer. Not only the ones about the boat explosion, but also the visions about Devon being abducted by his dad, and then taken to an island somewhere near Sitka.

Ty stood up. He seemed agitated. "What do we do now? We don't really know where to start looking for River, or even Devon."

Cassandra still looked like she was in shock. "I can't believe this. I'm standing here, talking to a real-life psychic... from Seattle. This is—amazing!"

Ty glared at her. "It will be amazing if she can find River."

I wrinkled my forehead. "Honestly, I don't know what to do next. I don't know where River is."

Pacing back and forth, Ty scowled. "We need to get a boat and go look for her!"

I shook my head. "No, we can't do that yet. I don't know where she is. We could be on the boat for days. If I don't know which direction she's in, I won't know where to look."

"If River is sending you messages through your drawings, Jenny, then you should draw," Cassandra said calmly.

We stared at her. "That's brilliant!" Ty broke into a wide smile. He shoved my sketchbook toward me. "Draw, Jenny."

I pushed the hair out of my face. "It's not that easy. I can't just draw on demand and expect to get results."

"Why not?" he asked.

"Trust me. I know from experience. The messages I'm getting about River have to happen organically—they can't be forced. Each time I've gotten a vision or have drawn something related to her, it happens when it wants to happen. Not when I try to force it."

"You have to try," Ty demanded. "This is important! She's been missing for almost two months."

"Okay, okay." Cassandra tried to calm him down. "Let's be logical about this. Why don't we give Jenny some breathing room. Class is almost over. We should really get our stuff together and head back. Maybe Jenny will get more information during the day in her other classes. Don't push her."

"Thank you, Cassandra," I said gratefully. "I'll do my best."

Ty turned his back on us and stalked off, leaving us alone.

"Boys!" Cassandra said under her breath. "They can be so impatient at times." She squinted at something toward the water. I followed her gaze and saw Kevin, who had wandered down the beach, and sat on a rock drawing some driftwood.

"Kevin from Ketchikan!" Cassandra shouted. "We have to get a move on!" She tore down the beach and hauled him up by the arm. Startled, he nearly fell over backward.

Even with all the drama of the morning, I smiled to myself. She sure had a way of breaking up the tension. She came bustling toward me, pushing Kevin forward the whole way.

I grabbed Kevin's arm and Cassandra grabbed his other one. "We're off to see the wizard," I sang. Cassandra quickly chimed in, and we made our way back to campus, Kevin trapped helplessly between us.

***

During lunch, Ty shot me anxious glances across the table.

"Nothing yet," I answered, without him even posing the question.

"Eat your fries." Cassandra pointed to Ty's plate. "Or I'll eat them for you."

Ty rolled his eyes and shoved the plate toward Cassandra. She pulled the plate closer, and selected the largest fry and dipped it into the ketchup.

I took a bite of my salad. My phone vibrated in my pocket. I pulled it out and looked at the screen. A text from Benny had arrived.

"GF, Frank is antsy. More visions of Devon."

"Like what?" I texted back.

"Devon's making a raft."

"I know," I replied.

"Frank says he's almost done but the raft won't hold."

"He might sink?"

"Yes. We need to hurry."

"What do you mean, we?" I texted, raising my eyebrows.

"We're coming up," Benny texted. "He's rented a boat."

"When?"

"Friday."

Friday! That was in a couple of days.

"Do you know where to find Devon?" I texted quickly.

"No. Frank said you should work on that. Gotta go. See you soon."

I slid my phone back in my pocket and looked up. Ty and Cassandra were staring at me. "What?" I took a sip of my water and tried to look normal.

"What's going on?" Cassandra asked.

"Friends from home are coming up to look for Devon." I shook my head. I still couldn't believe they were doing this.

"The missing kid?" Ty asked, a look of confusion crossing his face. "Why would they do that?"

"I met Frank and Benny in a class… a class to help develop psychic ability," I answered. "They're both psychic."

"OMG!" Cassandra shouted. "More psychics? They're coming here?"

"Shhh," I put my finger to my lips. "Yes, they're coming here. Frank's renting a boat."

"Is Frank your boyfriend?" asked Ty.

"No! Frank's old," I said indignantly.

"Is Benny your boyfriend?" Ty asked.

"No, Benny is gay."

"OMG, a gay psychic!" Cassandra said, clapping her hands gleefully. Several people sitting nearby gaped at us.

"Shhh!"

"Did they say anything about River?" Ty asked, ignoring Cassandra.

I shook my head.

His shoulders sank. I reached across the table and covered his hand with mine. "I'll try my best to find her."

Chapter 25

In poetry class, we were once again sent outside to get some inspiration from nature. Apparently our instructor, Branson, was big on the outdoors. Today's mission was to write a free verse poem.

I left the classroom, searching for a quiet place to write. Passing by the Yaw building, I noticed a gazebo next to a shallow creek. My footsteps sounded hollow as I crossed the wooden bridge over the stream. With no other campers in sight, this would be the perfect location. I sat down in the gazebo, and tried to make myself comfortable on the bench that skirted the inside of the structure.

The sound of the creek was soothing; the gurgling water caressed the rocks, plucking them like the strings of a guitar. I set the tip of the pencil on the paper, and tried to think of a good topic to write a poem about. Waiting for inspiration to strike, my eyelids became heavy. Sleep teased me as I listened to the water and the birds.

My chin dipped and hit my chest, and I jerked awake. Oh no! I had fallen asleep. I pulled my phone out to check the time. Class was almost over. Feeling foolish, and dreading the return to the classroom, I glanced down at my notebook. I couldn't believe it. I had written a poem. But I was asleep. How was that possible? I rubbed my eyes and looked at my notebook again.

Follow the raven
Through the sky,
Your sight will lead you to me.
In a protective cove,
I await your return,
And burning hearts will heal again.

I shook my head. What on earth? I thought back to the last poem I had written. I had thought it was about Mike. I was starting to think that it wasn't about him at all. The word "raven" appeared in that poem too. Obviously, this was a clue. But what did it mean?

Closing my notebook, I got up from the bench and stretched. A hummingbird darted past me and flitted to a nearby bush. All around me, nature hummed and buzzed. I left the gazebo and walked back to meet my classmates.

Just before I reached the building, a raven flew to the edge of the roof and peered down at me. Its black eyes gazed directly into mine. It nodded its shiny black head and leaped into the sky, looking back at me as it glided away.

***

Ty, Cassandra, and I met in the cafeteria after classes were over for the day.

"What's for dinner?" I asked.

Cassandra bounded over to the hot food section. "Spaghetti!" she yelled from across the room.

"Yum," I said. "Let's go sit over by the window."

We got our trays of food and sat down to eat.

"Did you learn anything new about River?" Ty asked after he took a bite of garlic bread.

I took a sip of my iced tea. "Yeah, I wrote a poem while I was sleeping in poetry class."

Cassandra grabbed my arm, causing my iced tea to spill over the lip of the glass. "You wrote a poem while you were sleeping?"

A puddle of tea spread out around my cup. I grabbed a napkin and began mopping it up. "It was the weirdest thing. I was really sleepy all of a sudden, and I nodded off. When I woke up, class was almost over. I looked at my notebook, and I had written a poem."

Ty stopped chewing and leaned forward. "What did the poem say?"

I opened the backpack by my feet and took out my notebook. "Actually, I have two poems. When I wrote the first one, I thought it was about something else. But now I think they are both related to River."

I handed the notebook over to Ty. He read the first poem out loud.

"On the wings of a raven,
I bid you farewell,
My friend I adored,
And loved you so well,
We will meet again soon,
In the golden light,
I won't rest well,
'Til you're in sight."
Flipping the page over, he read the next one.
"Follow the raven
Through the sky,
Your sight will lead you to me.
In a protective cove,
I await your return,
And burning hearts will heal again."

Cassandra's eyes were as wide as saucers. She snatched the notebook away from Ty, and reread the poems. "But what does it mean?" she whispered.

"It sounds like River is waiting for me to find her," Ty said.

I nodded. "But what does the raven reference mean? I've been seeing ravens or crows for the last month or so. Even in Seattle. It seems like too much of a coincidence, don't you think?

"Huh," Ty said. He took a bite of spaghetti and thought for a moment as he ate. "Both River and I are from the raven clan. It might have something to do with that."

"Raven clan?" I asked.

"Yeah, in the Tlingit culture there are clans. River and I are both ravens because our mothers are ravens. Children always take the clan of their mothers, since it's a matrilineal society."

I suddenly remembered what the Indian spirit said to me in Ketchikan, and gasped.

"What?" Cassandra said, watching my face.

"I just remembered something. I talked with a spirit in Ketchikan. He looked like an Indian chief or something."

Cassandra's eyes got wider.

"Anyway, he told me that the Tlingits in Sitka were expecting me, and that I should look for the one with the raven on his side."

"Oh my God. That's me." Ty said, startling both Cassandra and me.

"You?" Cassandra asked.

"The one with the raven on his side. That's me." He lifted his t-shirt up on his left side. The image of a raven spreading its wings was tattooed on his brown skin.

I gulped, looking at the magnificent bird. The tips of its wings rippled on his abs.

"I kind of believed my grandfather when he talked about you, but not completely. I mean, he's an old man, and his mind is not what it used to be. Sometimes, the old ways seem a little weird and crazy to me," he rambled. "But now, this is all starting to snap into place. Jenny, you were supposed to find me here all along. We're supposed to work together to find River."

"Yeah, I kind of got that," I said, unable to take my eyes off of his mid-section. "But I didn't know what the 'one with the raven on his side' meant until now. And I don't get how we'll find River. There must be hundreds of islands around here—hundreds of places we could search. But how will we know which island she's on? The picture I drew in class looks like it could be any island around here."

Ty shook his head. "Don't you realize how powerful your gift is? Grandfather told me stories about you. How your untapped energy could find River, and help so many other people. You have no idea…"

I shrugged. "I guess I don't. If I have this power, how will I know what to do with it?"

We fell silent for a moment. Then Cassandra piped up. "What do you normally do when you are stuck on something like this?"

Without giving it too much thought, I replied, "I meditate. I light a white candle, say a few prayers, and then ask Spirit to help me find the answer."

"Then that's what you need to do," she said simply.

I grinned. "You're really smart, Cassandra."

"I know." She winked. "We should get you to a quiet place where you can meditate right now. River can't wait forever for you to find her."

Ty nodded.

"I don't have a white candle or matches with me."

Cassandra looked at her watch. "It's only five o'clock. The stores are still open. Let's go get your supplies."

***

174

I sat on the floor of my room with the candle burning brightly in front of me. Cassandra and Ty took a walk so I could meditate in peace and quiet.

"Let the white light of the holy spirit surround and protect me," I prayed. "Spirit... God... please let me see what I need to do to find River." Then I thought about the little boy. "And please, help me find Devon."

Taking several deep breaths and blowing them out through my nose, I let my body relax. I pictured River in my head and concentrated on her face. Nothing. I tried relaxing even more. Maybe I could try Devon. I concentrated on him and took more breaths... in and out, in and out. Nothing. Opening my eyes, I stared at the white flame of the candle. The light flickered once, then once more.

Flash.

I spread my wings and jumped off the branch.

I took off over the water, where the green islands dotted the water below.

My eyes popped open. The raven! I remembered when I had become Kaya and had checked in on Mike. If I could see through the eyes of a dog, could I see through the eyes of a raven as well? And if I could see through the eyes of a raven, could it direct me to River or Devon? I couldn't wait to tell Cassandra and Ty about this.

I blew out the candle, gathered it up with the matches, and stood up. Placing the supplies on the dresser, I glanced into the mirror facing me and swiped a strand of hair off my face. Even if I doubted my ability, I had to try it.

My phone buzzed. A text from Mom.

"Just checking in. Having fun at camp?"

"Love it!" I texted back.

I stared at the screen, wondering if I should tell Mom about the new developments. She might overreact. I tried to put myself in her shoes. If my daughter told me that she would be getting on a boat with a couple of kids, an older

175

guy, and another kid from Seattle, to try and find missing people on random islands... No, I probably wouldn't encourage that.

"Need anything?" Mom texted.

"No, I'm fine."

"Ok, have fun!"

"Bye."

"Bye. Love you."

"Love you too." I felt slightly guilty for not telling her the whole story. I shoved my phone back in my pocket.

Chapter 26

There was a definite Friday vibe in the air. A volleyball net had been set up on the grass, and a group of kids were hitting a ball back and forth over the net at the beginning of the lunch hour. Cassandra, Ty and I decided to leave campus and eat in town.

We walked past the light gray onion-domed church in the center of town, and I turned to look up at it.

"This is pretty." I shaded my eyes from the sun as I squinted at the diagonal cross on top of the dome.

"St. Michael's Cathedral," Cassandra said. "It's a Russian Orthodox church."

"The Russians sure had a lot of influence here," I said.

"Yeah," she replied. "I can't think of any other town in America where Russian culture has had so much impact."

"Can we go in?" I asked.

"Sure," Ty answered. We checked to make sure that no cars were coming and crossed the narrow road to the steps of the church. The doors were open. Inside the entrance, there was a donation box, a guest book, and glass cases containing elaborately embellished gold-leafed bibles. A few silver and gold crosses were propped up inside the cases as well.

The inner doors to the sanctuary looked to be plated in real gold. Six panels opened up on the doors, depicting saints. Their portraits were painted in oil and decorated in gold relief. We went inside, and peered into the small church. The inside looked like a scaled-down version of a European cathedral. The walls and floors were all white, with gold trim everywhere. More paintings adorned the walls, each framed in thick gold. Everywhere, gold bowl-like chandeliers hung from the ceiling. White candles inside the bowls were lit and shimmered in the brightness of the church.

"I was not expecting this," I said in an awed whisper.

Ty nodded and moved closer to me. "It's pretty cool, huh? I guess I kind of take it for granted, having lived here all my life. I hardly ever come in here."

I stepped closer to one of the paintings on the wall, and examined the angel with white feathery wings and a significant gold halo around her head. A saint, also with a halo around his head, stood to the right of the angel. I stared at the saint's face. Suddenly, the image blurred, almost as if the paint was rearranging itself. I watched until the face came back into focus… the face of River appeared in its place.

"Oh!"

Ty came up behind me and looked at the painting. "Something wrong?"

"The saint! Look at the face—it's River."

He shook his head. "No, it's an old guy."

I rubbed my eyes. He was right—the face wasn't River's. I turned to Ty. "What is River's connection to Russian culture?"

He blinked.

"Ty, what is River's last name?"

Cassandra and Ty answered at the same time. "Lisyansky."

"Russian?"

Ty nodded. "Her dad has Russian ancestry."

"What happened to him? Is he still alive?"

"Yeah, he is. He was on the boat when it exploded. He was thrown into the water, but he was really lucky to have been rescued by a fishing boat a little while later."

"And there was no sign of River?"

"Or her mom," Cassandra added. "It was a miracle that Mr. Lisyansky was found."

I tried to process the information. "Do the authorities know the cause of the explosion?"

"Tom—that's River's dad, said that he was having engine trouble. He's a smoker, and while he was working on the engine, some ashes from his cigarette ignited the fuel."

My heart started to thump in my chest. Something was all wrong about this. "How do you feel about him?"

"What do you mean?" Ty asked.

"I mean, is he a good guy?"

"If you're asking if I think he killed River and my aunt, then my answer is, no, I don't think that's possible. He's an okay guy. He was completely torn up after the accident."

"The police did an investigation and cleared him," Cassandra said. "There was an article about it in the paper."

But I couldn't ignore the hairs on the back of my neck—which were standing at full attention.

I blew out a loud sigh. "Something about this is not quite right."

"Jenny, I don't think so." Ty took my arm and led me out of the church. Cassandra followed behind us. "Let's go grab something to eat at the coffee shop and head back to campus. I'll tell you more about him on the way."

***

179

We walked down the sidewalk, munching on our sandwiches and sipping our iced teas.

"Do you know Tom well?" I asked.

"Yeah, I guess," he answered. "They live right next door to me. My uncle travels a lot for work, so I've never spent a lot of time with him. He and River had an okay relationship as far as fathers and daughters go."

"What about his relationship with your aunt?"

He shrugged. "Okay, I guess. I mean, they seemed more like roommates rather than husband and wife."

I stopped walking. Cassandra collided into me, nearly dropping her sandwich.

"Sorry!" I said as I helped to steady her.

"Geez, Jenny. I almost lost my lunch. Oh! Lost my lunch. Ha, that's funny!" she giggled. "You know, as in throwing up… tossing my cookies. Get it?"

Ty rolled his eyes and made an effort to ignore Cassandra. "Something wrong?" He stared at me intently.

"Everything you've said about your uncle… the word 'okay' came up a couple of times. He's an 'okay' guy. His relationship with River is 'okay.' Not to mention that his relationship with his wife seems rather unexciting."

"What are you trying to say?"

I bit my lip. "I'm just saying, I think something is wrong here. I don't just think it, I feel it. Where is your uncle? Can I meet him?"

Ty shook his head. "He left town. The accident really messed him up. He spent weeks out on his friend's boat, searching for River and his wife. When nothing turned up, he left town—couldn't stand to live in the house with all those memories."

I swallowed hard. "Where did he go?"

Ty frowned. "I'm not sure. Seattle, I think."

"Seattle," Cassandra echoed.

Suddenly, my head spun. The memory of Celine's class field trip into Pioneer Square popped into my head.

The man who appeared in color to me, when everyone else, was dimmed to black and white.

The crows swooping down off the trees to attack them.

The crows... ravens.

"Oh my God!" I yelled.

Cassandra jumped, spilling her tea all over her jeans. "Not again," she sighed.

"What?" Ty asked anxiously.

"Is your uncle in his mid-fifties, with sandy-blond hair? About twenty pounds over-weight?"

Ty's eyebrows shot upward. "Yeah! Wait—what's going on? What did you see?"

I explained what happened in Celine's class on our field trip.

"No way!" Cassandra shouted.

Ty's mouth hung open. "Are you sure?" He paced back and forth. "Do you really think he had something to do with this?"

"Yes, I do."

"Should we call the police?" Cassandra took her cell phone out of her pocket and tapped the screen.

"Not the local police," I said. "I'll call Detective Coalfield in Seattle. I've worked with him before, and I trust him completely."

Cassandra's eyes bugged out of her head. "God," she whispered. "You are hands down the coolest friend I have ever had."

As we walked back toward campus, the familiar sound of drumming I'd first heard the day I visited Pioneer Square filled my ears.

Chapter 27

"Detective Coalfield?"

"Yes, Jenny?"

"I have some information for you."

"About Devon?"

"Well, sort of."

Ty and Cassandra were sitting on the floor, leaning their backs against my bunk, looking anxious.

"There is a girl and her mom that were in a boat accident... an explosion. I think I know where to find them."

"I'm afraid I can't help you with that one, Jenny. That's not in my jurisdiction. You'll have to call the Sitka police department."

"Wait!" I said, a little too loudly. "There's something else. Devon has been making a raft. We don't think it will hold him—and if he escapes off the island, he may drown."

"Whoa, whoa, whoa!" the detective said. "Back up a little. First of all, who is 'we'?"

I explained about my psychic friends, and how they were flying up to Alaska to join me and Cassandra and Ty.

"So, this Frank guy has been picking up vibes on Devon too?"

"Yeah, he is. He and Benny are flying up here this afternoon. Frank has rented a boat. We're all going out this weekend to try and find Devon, River, and her mom."

There was silence on the other end of the line.

"Detective?"

"Yep, I'm here."

"There's more. River's dad survived the boat explosion. The police have cleared him and ruled it as an accident. But I really and truly believe that he did this on purpose."

He let out a low whistle. "Sounds like you are opening a can of worms here, Jenny—especially if he's already been cleared of any wrong-doing."

I explained that I saw the man in Seattle and the circumstances behind it. "Just so you know, his name is Tom Lisyansky," I said. I asked Ty to spell it for me and then relayed it to the detective. "Can you just try and look him up on your end to see if you discover anything odd about him?"

"Tell you what," he said. "I'll have someone look into that. But since you are going to be out looking for Devon, and he's under *my* jurisdiction, I'm taking the next flight up there. I sure hope you have room for me on that boat of yours." He hung up.

I looked at my phone with amazement and shoved it back in my pocket.

"What?" Ty asked. He jumped up from the floor.

"Detective Coalfield is coming on the next flight up here," I stammered.

Cassandra bounced up from her seated position and grabbed my arms. "OMG! Is he coming on the boat with us?"

I nodded. "Yeah, he is."

"I've got to go talk to Grandfather," Ty announced. "He can get the entire Tlingit community behind us— especially the raven clan shamans and elders."

"The one with the raven on his side," I repeated what the spirit in Ketchikan said.

My phone buzzed. I took it out of my pocket and looked at the screen.

"It's Benny," I said. "He and Frank have just landed." I texted him back. "Do you need a ride?"

"No. Frank is renting a car."

"Where do you want to meet?"

"Meet us for dinner in an hour at the Westmark Hotel."

***

"Benny!" I shouted, spotting him in the hotel lobby. I ran to greet him and threw my arms around him. "It's so great to see you."

He grinned, looking sheepish. "You too."

Frank stood behind Benny. I unwrapped my arms from around him and stood on my toes to hug Frank.

"Hello, young lady," he said.

"Benny, Frank—these are my friends, Ty and Cassandra," I said motioning to them. "They know all about what's going on."

"Nice to meet you," Frank said. "Are they coming with us tomorrow?"

I nodded.

"Good thing I rented a large boat," Frank answered. "I had a feeling there would be more of us."

"Well, you were right!" Cassandra added. "And there is one more joining us. A detective from Seattle."

"Are you kidding?" Benny seemed taken aback. Even Frank looked surprised.

"No, we're not kidding," I answered. "Detective Coalfield is the guy I worked with on Callie Shoemaker's case."

"And he's involved in Devon's situation?" Frank asked.

"Only because I involved him." I told them how I had engaged the detective when I had my first vision of the little boy being abducted in Renton. "He works for the Bellevue police, but got assigned to the case when he started getting more information from me."

"Let's talk more while we eat." Frank ushered us down the hall.

I laughed out loud when I saw the name of the restaurant. "The Raven Dining Room? You've got to be kidding me."

The hostess seated us at a large table overlooking the corner of Lincoln Street and Harbor Drive. We had a peek-a-boo view of Crescent Harbor from our table. The dark wood interior reminded me of a ski lodge—big heavy timbers lined the high ceilings above us, and rich coffee-colored floors lay beneath our feet. There were a few other groups of people eating, but none of them near our table.

We ordered our food and while we waited for it to come, Frank took out some maps and unfolded them on the table.

"I picked up some charts on the way here." He smoothed the papers out and we all leaned over them. "I'm a little nervous because I don't know these waters."

"I do," Ty said. "I can captain the boat if you want."

"Do you have a boat?" Frank asked. "I could've saved myself the rental."

"I just have a seventeen-foot Boston Whaler," Ty answered. "It would never hold six people…three maybe, but not six."

Frank chuckled. "It's no problem, actually. Like I said, I was expecting there to be more people than just Jenny."

"So, what's our plan?" Cassandra asked. "How do we know which of these islands to search?"

Everyone looked at me expectantly. "Oh, uh—I think that's why we're all here. But, I believe it might help seeing through the eyes of a raven."

"Huh?" Benny looked at me funny.

I described how I was able to see through a dog's eyes, and how I dreamt of seeing through a raven's eyes.

"Geez!" The surprised look on Benny's face made me laugh. "You can really do that? Your psychic talent far surpasses mine."

"Have you tried it on a raven yet?" Frank asked.

"No, just in my dream. But I'm pretty sure it will work. We'll have to give it a try. Otherwise, we'll just be taking a stab in the dark," I replied.

Frank nodded. "Since I've been getting visions of Devon, I can try to get more visual details about the island he's on."

"If you combine your talents," Ty said, "you might be able to find everyone."

"But who do we look for first?" Cassandra said.

"River," Ty said at the same time Frank answered, "Devon." They glared at each other for a moment.

"So," I said quickly, "let's kind of play this by ear. Let the spirits guide us and they can decide who we find first."

Ty shrugged. "If you think that's best, then okay."

Frank grumbled a little, but gave in.

The waitress arrived with a big tray of food that she set up on a rack next to our table. She set my grilled king salmon and steamed vegetables in front of me. Cassandra looked blissful as she squirted ketchup onto her plate full of piping hot french fries and fried fish.

"Fish and chips?" I asked. "Is that cod?"

"Nope." She mopped a trickle of grease from the corner of her mouth. "Halibut."

We all dug into our food. I could almost see the wheels turning in everyone's brains while we chewed.

"When does the detective get here?" Frank asked.

"Whenever the next flight arrives." I took the last bite of my salmon.

"Then he'll get here late this evening." Frank said. "The next flight arrives at 10:54 p.m."

"Should we meet with him tonight?" Cassandra's face glowed with excitement. "We should pick him up at the airport!"

"The sooner, the better," Frank said. "We need to have our plan in place by tomorrow morning."

I took my phone out and texted Detective Coalfield. "Are you on the late flight? We can pick you up at the airport."

"Listen," said Frank. "We need to get some supplies for the boat tomorrow. I'll take Benny and Cassandra to the grocery store to get some snacks and drinks. Jenny, you and Ty should pick up some flares, and two more life jackets. The rental only comes with four of those."

"Can we get life jackets late at night? It's after six o'clock."

"I've got extra at home," Ty said. "No need to buy them. I don't have any flares, though. I'm pretty sure I saw some at Sea Mart."

"Sea Mart?" Benny asked.

"It's a grocery store, but they carry other stuff too. How about if you guys go there to get the food and the flares?" Ty pushed his plate away, and pulled out his cell phone. "I'm going to tell Grandfather what's going on." He got up from the table, and went out of the dining area and into the hall.

My phone buzzed. Detective Coalfield had texted back.

"Just about to get on the plane. A ride would be nice. Staying at the Westmark."

I smiled. He must be psychic too—he picked the same hotel as Frank and Benny. "See you later."

187

Frank gathered up his charts and folded them. He took the check from the waitress and handed her his credit card. She was back a moment later and he signed his name on the bill.

"Thanks for buying." Cassandra said, patting her stomach. "That was a great meal, but I ate too much. You'll have to roll me out of here."

He helped her out of her chair. "Come on, kids, let's go get our stuff. Cassandra, you'll have to give me directions to Sea Mart."

We met Ty in the hall. "Grandfather wants us all to meet at his house right after we pick up Detective Coalfield."

"What for?" Benny asked.

"I don't know—he said something about aligning our totem animals or something like that."

Frank groaned. "This is going to be a long night. Theoretically, we should all be up at the crack of dawn to get on the boat."

"The crack of dawn is around four o'clock in the morning this time of year," Ty said. "Do you really want to get up that early? We might as well not go to bed."

"Shoot. I forgot about the Alaskan summers and how much light you get up here," Frank grumbled. "We'll definitely need some sleep before we head out. Let's get a move on so we can be ready by the time we go to the airport."

Chapter 28

"Good thing your house is close to downtown," I said as we turned the corner.

"It's convenient. Can you text the others, and tell them to meet us in the Sea Mart parking lot?" He looked at his watch. "In about an hour?"

"Sure." I dug the phone out of my pocket and attempted to text while I walked. We reached Ty's house just as I finished. His house was a small one-story home, painted white with dark blue trim. We opened the little picket fence gate and walked up the path.

"Mom should be home from work now." He unlocked the door and went inside.

"Ty? Is that you?"

"Yeah, it's me." He shut the door behind us. Ty's mom came out of the kitchen. She was wearing an apron with a Tlingit design of a salmon on the front. A delicious chocolate smell drifted out of the kitchen.

She was short and had long dark hair and a heart-shaped face. Her brown eyes were warm just like her son's. Even though she was smiling, a heavy sense of sadness surrounded her and showed in the lines on her face. "Is this Jenny?" She approached me hesitantly. "I'm Gwen."

"I'm Jenny. Nice to meet you, Gwen." I held my hand out to shake hers.

She bypassed my hand and stepped in to hug me tightly. "Thank you," she whispered. "Thank you for trying to help find my sister and niece."

I felt her sadness and grief—it was almost too much to bear. I took in a sharp breath and said to myself, *let the white light of the holy spirit surround and protect me.* I needed to keep her feelings separate from mine so I could do my job to find her loved ones.

"Come sit down," she said, pointing to a worn floral-patterned sofa. The timer beeped, and she walked into the kitchen. "I need to get that. Be right back."

Ty took my hand. "Are you okay?"

"Yeah, sure." I glanced down at his hand covering mine. I felt a little self-conscious. Was he holding my hand because he liked me or because he was trying to reassure me? Was I cheating on Mike? I pushed the thought away. Mike dumped me. Even if Ty kissed me, I wasn't cheating on Mike because I was no longer his girlfriend.

Gwen came out of the kitchen holding something wrapped in aluminum foil. "Cookies," she said, "for your boat trip."

Ty took them and placed them on the coffee table in front of us. "Thank you, Mom."

"Aren't you going to have one?" she asked.

"Not right now. We ate at the Westmark. Hey, I need to grab two lifejackets. The boat we're renting only has four."

"There are six of you?"

I gave her a brief explanation of all that happened today.

"My God!" Her hand covered her mouth in surprise. "You mean, Tom did this? He took Cathy and River?"

"I know it sounds crazy," Ty said. "I didn't believe it at first either. But everything that Jenny said makes sense. It had to be him."

"And you're going to find the little boy in the same trip?" she asked. "What if he's in a completely different area?"

Ty shrugged. "I don't know how that's going to work out. But it's reassuring to have the detective, Frank, Benny, and Cassandra with us."

"It makes me feel better to know you'll have some adults with you." She grabbed a small notepad from the coffee table and scribbled something down. She ripped the paper off and handed it to Ty. "You'll need permission to leave the campus this weekend."

"Yeah, you're right." He pocketed the note. "I'll turn this into the counselor tomorrow."

I realized with horror, that I would also need consent. "What am I going to do? I'll have to tell my parents something to get permission."

"Just tell them that you got invited to go on a boat trip with some friends," Ty said.

I got up from the couch. "I guess we'd better get going."

"Hold on," Gwen said. "I'll get those lifejackets for you." She left the room and went out to the enclosed back porch. "Here you go," she said as she came back. "These are pretty small, so they should work for the girls."

Ty took the lifejackets from her and gave his mom a hug. "Love you, Mom."

"Love you too, Ty Ty."

We left the house and went down the stairs. "Ty Ty?" I asked with a grin.

"Shut up," he said. His shy smile made him even more endearing to me.

While Ty drove, I texted my parents the scoop about the boat trip.

"Okay, I'll call the camp to let them know," Mom texted.

"Thanks, Mom."

"Have fun. Be safe."

I put my phone away. "Hey, wasn't that Sea Mart we just passed?" I pointed to the left. The store was on the water's edge. Only in Alaska would they put a grocery store on prime waterfront property.

"Yeah, but we still have twenty minutes before we're supposed to meet them. I thought we'd drive to Sandy Beach. It's not far."

A few minutes later, we pulled into a small parking lot. The truck was facing Sitka Sound, and the view was spectacular. Mt. Edgecumbe, the volcano, was plainly visible across the water, its top highlighted with a few lingering streaks of snow. Ty rolled the windows down, and a fresh sea breeze drifted through the cab of the truck. It was well after nine o'clock, and the sun was just now beginning its slow descent to the horizon line.

"Here we are. Sandy Beach."

"That's it?" The sandy part was tiny—maybe a quarter of the length of a football field, if that.

"It's not much, but it's scenic, isn't it?"

I turned my gaze back to the water. The sound of the waves crashing on the shore was soothing. The sky had turned the color of peaches, and the clouds were streaked with raspberry. I was in awe. "It's beautiful."

While Ty watched a seagull fly over the iridescent water, I snuck a peek at his profile. His strong features were tempered with a boyish softness. He was handsome and cute at the same time. Suddenly, I felt nervous and self-conscious being near him… just like I did around Mike when we first started dating.

"It's going to get crazy tomorrow, isn't it?" he said quietly, turning his face to me.

I shivered, thinking about all that would happen. We were about to embark on a crazy boat trip—looking for River, her mom, and Devon. What if we didn't find them? Worse yet, what if we found them, but they were dead?

"Are you cold?" Ty wrapped his arm around me and scooted me toward him on the truck's bench seat.

"A little." The cold wasn't what was making me shake.

He pulled me closer to him. "How's that?"

"Better," I mumbled.

"Jenny?" I could feel his breath on my neck.

"Tell me about River," I blurted out as I jerked slightly away from him. My nerves had me trembling too hard. I needed to deflect how I felt about Ty for a moment while I gathered my thoughts.

"Oh, uh—she's really nice." He sighed. "She talks way too much—drives me nuts sometimes. She has a wicked sense of humor though. The stuff we used to pull when we were kids!" He laughed. "Actually, she and I are more like brother and sister than cousins."

"Really?" I thought of my cousins who lived in Puyallup. I didn't get to see them much. I loved hanging out with them, but we weren't as close as siblings for sure. Not that I was close to Jackson.

"She and Aunt Cathy live right next door to us. When my dad died, Mom had to go back to work. I spent most of my time at their house. River and I would get into all sorts of trouble—her ideas of course." His eyes twinkled.

"Of course." It was so sweet to hear him talk about his cousin. I remembered that he still had his arm around me, and I got nervous all over again.

"You okay?" he asked.

"Yes." I stared out the window. I could sense him looking at me.

"Jenny, I know we had some time to kill, but I really brought you here because I wanted to share a moment with you before... you know, before tomorrow."

I turned to look at him.

"Like I said, it's going to get crazy. There will be a lot going on. I just wanted to..." He brushed the hair off my shoulder.

My heart galloped in my chest. He leaned in and very gently, brushed his lips against mine.

"You're shaking," he whispered. "Should I roll up the window?"

I shook my head. "It's not that. It's..." I turned my face up to his, biting my lip.

His eyebrows arched in surprise. "I'm making you nervous, aren't I?"

I nodded.

"I thought it was the other way around!" He looked into my eyes. "I guess we have the same effect on each other." He leaned in and kissed me again. This time, I kissed him back, my heart thudding in my chest.

Smiling, he opened the door and pulled me out of the truck. "Come on. We have a few minutes. Let's go down to the beach."

My body was still jittery from the kiss. He grabbed my hand and we climbed over the rocks until our feet were on the sand. The sky was turning an intense orange, still laced with pink clouds, the colors deepening as we watched the horizon.

"Do you think she's out there?" His expression was hopeful and sad at the same time.

I thought of River and her mom. I knew they were out there—I just wasn't sure if they were alive. Ty looked so expectant... I didn't want to crush him. "Yes. Yes, I think she's out there."

Grabbing my hands, he pulled me toward him. He tilted my face up to his and kissed me. His lips lingered on

194

mine. Sadness rolled off his body in waves. Yet there was another emotion there, too—passion. It was almost as if he needed to forget the worries of what had happened to his cousin and aunt, and to lose himself in the moment. Kissing him was exhilarating. He draped his arms around me and drew me in closer. I could feel his heart beating and my heart began to match the beat of his.

Suddenly, unwelcome images of Mike surfaced in my mind—Mike kissing me on the beach in West Seattle. Mike and I kissing by Snoqualmie Falls, the roar of water in my ears. I pulled away.

"Is something wrong?"

"No. I just have a lot on my mind. You know, about tomorrow."

He nodded. "Believe me, I know how you feel. Let's drive over to Sea Mart." He took my hand and we walked back up the beach. "The others might be done shopping by now."

As we walked, I wondered why on earth I would be thinking about Mike. Ty was awesome. He was handsome, sweet, and protective—all the things I could ever want in a boyfriend. Maybe it was because I knew that only a week from now, I would be going back to Seattle, and he would be staying here. Whatever the reason was, I was disappointed in myself. This guy was making my pulse race and leaving me feeling weak at the knees with each kiss. So, why was I still thinking about Mike?

Chapter 29

We had picked up the detective at the airport, and were gathered on the front porch of Ty's grandfather's house. It was almost midnight so we tried not to make much noise.

A slightly-built old man opened the door. "You're here." It was stated matter-of-factly. He hugged his grandson and welcomed us into his home. "Come into the kitchen. I have some coffee for you. Don't worry," he added. "It's decaf." His voice was velvety and rich.

"Where's Grandma?" Ty looked around.

"She's been asleep for hours. She's not a night-owl like you and me."

The kitchen was small, but very tidy. The aroma of coffee drifted through the air and created a cozy atmosphere. The old man had moved the kitchen table and chairs against the wall, so there was more room to stand. Cups, sugar, and cream had been set on the counter, and a coffee pot was percolating next to them.

"Everyone, this is my grandfather, Henry."

Henry smiled. "Hello."

"Grandfather, this is Cassandra, Frank, Benny, Detective Coalfield, and Jenny." Ty pointed to each of us as he spoke.

Henry's eyes settled on me, and he stepped forward. "Jenny. We've been waiting a long time to meet you. Thank you for coming. Thank you *all* for coming to help find my daughter and granddaughter." He cleared his throat. "I'm sure you're wondering why I called you here so late at night. I know you will be out on a boat tomorrow. But before you go, I would like to align your totem animals. You will need their help on your journey."

"Totem animals?" Benny fidgeted with the zipper on his hoodie. "What does that mean?"

The old man continued. "Everyone has at least one, if not more, totem animals. They are the spirits of animals who are your allies while you are here on this earth plane. Tlingits don't necessarily believe in spirit animals. But as a young man and a shaman, I traveled the world, and have met with spiritual leaders from many different places. Among them, it is a common belief that we have at least one spirit animal. They leave you signs. They help guide you. All you have to do is listen. Listen and watch. Keep your mind open."

"Even white people?" Cassandra asked innocently. "We have totem animals too?"

Henry laughed, a gurgle that slowly worked its way out to a loud guffaw. "Yes, child. We are all one, don't you see? We are all connected. It doesn't matter if you are Tlingit, or Jewish, Arabic, or any other culture or religion. Simply put, we come here with unseen helpers: angels, totem animals, the spirits of those who have passed into the next life. We could not survive without their support."

"Geesh," Cassandra murmured. "That is freakin' awesome."

"They give us the power to heal." He glanced at Ty.

I remembered the day I had twisted my ankle at Totem Park—Ty's hands had seemed hot on my skin, and the pain had gone away so quickly.

"They give us the power to help one another. Some of us have had many, many lives and in those lives, we have developed our gifts over time. You," he said, taking my hand, "have had numerous past lives. In each one, you have been a seer, a shaman, and a healer. Your power has built up after so many centuries and is so great. You don't seem to know it." He smiled at me affectionately. "That is why I called you here. Your father had a burning desire to come to Alaska on a boat. Why do you think that happened? This is how our lives are intertwined. There is a reason for everything."

This was unreal.

"So, it is late. Please, everyone, help yourselves to a little coffee and let's get started."

We drank our coffee quickly and talked in hushed voices.

"This is so wild," Benny said under his breath.

"I know." I took a sip of coffee. "I almost need a day to let this all soak in."

"But we don't have a day." Benny took the last swig of his drink. "We start in just a few hours."

"All right," Henry announced. "Form a circle, please."

We arranged ourselves. Ty stood on one side of me, Benny on the other.

Henry went back into the room behind the kitchen and came out with a drum. He began chanting in a language that I didn't understand. The chanting and drumming reminded me of the drumming I'd heard in Pioneer Square.

Suddenly, Ty's grandmother, wrapped in a robe, stumbled sleepily into the kitchen. "What a ruckus!" she said. Henry smiled at her and continued to drum as she slipped in next to him. She joined in the chanting as if this was an everyday occurrence.

Within a few minutes, I began to see a white vapor building in the center of our circle. One by one, our animal totems emerged, and whirled around in the center before

198

joining their corresponding human. First, a shimmering white doe lifted from the center, spun around Cassandra, and then stood at her side. She nearly swooned as she stared at her spirit animal. Next, an eagle soared upward, unfolded its wings and landed on Detective Coalfield's shoulder. Surprisingly, everyone seemed to be seeing the totem animals—even those who were not psychic.

A big grizzly bear arose next, swirling around Frank and landing by his side. Frank stared at it in awe. Benny watched in horror as a rabbit bounded out from the circle and hopped over to him. "Isn't it bad enough that I had to be the skinny gay kid? Why do I have to have a stupid bunny as an animal totem?" he hissed.

I stifled a snort and elbowed him. "You have to admit," I whispered. "It's pretty adorable."

At last, two ravens emerged from the swirling mist. One circled around Ty's head and landed on his shoulder, and the other on mine. Ty and I exchanged a glance. We had the same totem animals. The deeper we got into this, the more I realized that I was not in charge—the coincidences were too great to just be coincidences. We were carefully placed together to resolve this situation—like two pawns in a chess game controlled by the universe.

Henry and his wife's chanting intensified. The animals suddenly left our sides, swirled above our heads, and disappeared into thin air. The drumming stopped abruptly and Henry nodded solemnly at us. "It is done. Your animals are aligned and ready to serve you on your journey tomorrow."

"How does that work?" Detective Coalfield asked.

"Each animal has attributes that will aid you. The deer," he said, looking at Cassandra, "is sure-footed and agile. It will help you stay on the path."

She smiled and nodded.

Henry glanced at Detective Coalfield. "The eagle is courageous and masculine—he takes charge and protects." He continued on. "Now Frank, you have the bear. He is protective too, but he is creative as well, and possesses the power to heal."

Benny's shoulders slumped.

"You may think the rabbit is harmless and weak, but in actuality, it is as quick as lightning, and able to dodge its enemies with a flick of its tail." Henry said with a smile. "Never underestimate any creature. They all have their strengths. It is important to value them for what they are."

Ty and I looked expectantly at his grandfather. Henry cleared his throat. "And last, but not least, the raven. In our culture, our ancestors believed that the raven created this world. With each drop of water that dripped from the bird's beak, an ocean, river, or lake emerged on the earth below. The raven is magic. Cunning, swift, and stealthy, the raven knows when to use its powers. He always wins against his enemies."

A rush surged through my veins. I felt the magic of the words—the magic of the raven.

Ty stepped forward and hugged his grandparents tightly. "Thank you for helping us."

Henry smiled sadly. "You will need all the help you can get, I'm afraid."

Chapter 30

It was seven o'clock in the morning and the boat was loaded with snacks, drinks, and first aid supplies. Frank had rented a fifty-two foot motor boat which included an inflatable dinghy that was attached to the side for going ashore if needed.

"This must have cost you a fortune!" I noted the size of the boat—so much bigger than the vessel we had taken to Sitka.

"When you don't have a family to spend it on," he replied, "you find yourself with more money than one person can spend. It's okay, I wanted to do this."

"Thanks, Frank," the detective said. "By the way, I let the Coast Guard and the local police know that we're out searching today."

"You did?" Benny seemed surprised. "Are they going to follow us?"

"No," he answered with a laugh. "I think they thought I was a bit of a nut ball. I made the mistake of mentioning that I'd received a tip from a psychic."

"I thought you said that a lot of people in the police force use psychics from time to time," I said.

"They do, but they usually keep it to themselves. No one wants to look like they believe in that sort of thing. If you tell a group of people on the force that you're acting on information from a psychic, they'll pretend you're crazy and write you off."

"But they work with psychics on their own and don't tell anyone?" Ty asked.

"Ironic, isn't it?" the detective said.

"Screw them. Let's get a move on." Frank started the motor and slowly navigated the way out of the harbor. Detective Coalfield joined him in the cabin. The rest of us sat on the aft deck of the boat on cream-colored waterproof cushions, too tired to make conversation. The skin under Cassandra's eyes was puffy, and for once, she was silent.

Ty rummaged through a cardboard box next to the seats and brought out a large thermos, a stack of paper cups, cream, and sugar.

"Thank God," mumbled Benny. He took a cup and Ty poured some coffee for him. Benny squinted into the cup. "Is it my imagination, or is this only half full?"

Ty shook his head. "We've got to ration the coffee. There are six of us that need to wake up. Someone will get cheated out of a drink if I give you a full cup's worth."

"Dude, I'm from Seattle," Benny muttered under his breath. "This is just an appetizer." He swirled the dark liquid around in his cup like a wine connoisseur.

"Why don't you add in some cream?" Ty grinned. "It'll trick your brain into thinking there's more."

Benny sighed dramatically and poured in some cream and a packet of sugar.

Soon, we all had our coffee and were looking a little more alive.

In addition to the drinks, there were a couple of boxes of doughnuts from the grocery store bakery. I bit into my old-fashioned glazed donut and chewed slowly, savoring the rush of sugar and carbs.

We had meandered out of the harbor and were now headed out into Sitka Sound.

"Now what?" Cassandra asked. She finished her doughnut, licked the sugar off her fingers and reached into the box for another one.

"Now we figure out which direction to head in," I answered.

"How do we do that?" she asked.

Frank cut the engine, and he and the detective came out to join us on deck. "Let's discuss our options." He took out the nautical charts he had shown us the night before.

"Where was your uncle found after the boat accident?" Detective Coalfield asked Ty. "It seems like it would be the place to start. Unless any of you guys have picked up on Devon's location."

"All I know is that Devon is on an island somewhere." I sipped my coffee. "Frank, did you get anything on Devon in your visions?"

"No. Just that he was building a raft. Let's go with Ty's knowledge of where his uncle was found first. Maybe something will come to me on the way there."

"Well," Ty said as he inspected the map. "He was rescued right about here." He pointed to an area on the map where there was a large, open expanse of water. Further away, was a group of islands clustered together like pebbles.

"Did anyone search those?" Frank asked.

"Sure," Cassandra said. "They searched everywhere for days."

"They just couldn't find anything," Ty said. His voice cracked and he swallowed hard. I grabbed his hand and squeezed it. His eyes met mine, and he looked away quickly. "I mean, they found some boat debris from the explosion, but there was no evidence of either my aunt or my cousin anywhere."

"This happened a couple of months ago. The temperature was still pretty cold. If you fall in the water here, you don't have much time to survive. It's just too frigid." Cassandra's eyes dropped to her shoes.

"I still think there is a chance that they made it." Ty's face hardened with resolve. "And if they are out there, we will find them."

"Of course we will," I said. The gnawing feeling in my stomach gurgled up. I swallowed hard to suppress it.

"Ty, come into the cabin and get us to that spot on the map where your uncle was found," Frank said. "We'll figure out what to do from there."

The sky was blue, but a few clouds had moved in, and the wind had picked up a little. An hour passed by quietly. Seagulls followed the boat, hoping for a handout of bait or a leftover doughnut. Their calls floated above us and were carried away by the breeze. I crossed my arms and rubbed them for warmth.

The water churned around the engine, leaving a white wake behind. We were approaching a cluster of islands. Some were small and some rather large. Suddenly, the engine cut and the water was still. The echo of the engine noise ricocheted off the land around us.

Ty, Frank, and Detective Coalfield joined us on the aft deck.

"Here we are," Frank said gruffly.

"But where do we start?" Cassandra turned and looked at me expectantly.

I chewed on my lip, and sorted through options of what we would do next. Should we start searching each island methodically? That could take all day. Maybe if we closed our eyes and meditated we could decide which island to search first? I noticed a raven flying to the port side of the boat. I knew what to do.

"Remember how I can inhabit an animal's body?"

"Are you thinking of trying that now?" Ty asked. "What if it doesn't work?"

"I've been able to do that in a dog's body, but I've never tried inhabiting a bird's." I pointed up to the raven. "If I can look through the eyes of that raven, maybe I can direct it toward the islands and can get a bird's-eye view. I might even be able to see if there are people below."

"Is that dangerous?" Frank asked.

"I have no idea."

"What happens to *your* body when you leave it?" Cassandra asked.

"I don't know exactly. The only time I tried it, I was sitting on a boat and when I came back to my body, I was still in the same position."

"Let's have you sit over here then, so you don't fall into the water when you try it." Ty put his arm around my waist and led me to the bank of cushions. "I'll sit right next to you to keep you safe."

I smiled and leaned into him.

His arm curled protectively around my shoulders. "Are you ready?"

I looked around at everyone's concerned faces. "Yes, I'm ready." Tilting my face skyward, I concentrated on the raven as it flew overhead. I tried to imagine becoming the bird and the view it would have from above.

Nothing happened for a moment, but then a funny tingling feeling started in my stomach. I felt myself pulling out of my body and being swept upward. This was like going on a ride at the fair—the kind where you were pulled straight up a tall narrow shaft and then dropped from a perilous height, your stomach threatening to exit through your mouth.

I leveled off, travelling horizontally rather than vertically. I wobbled, trying to straighten out. The boat was floating down below me. I was flying! Glancing below again, I could see myself surrounded by my group of friends, all watching me on the deck. Euphoria and adrenaline surged through me. I wanted to swoop down around them to see the looks on their faces. But I couldn't control this body. It was going where it was going, and I had to go along for the ride.

My wings flapped, and the breeze tickled my feathers. I gave into the feeling of being weightless, enjoying the freedom. Where was I headed? I craned my neck and looked down at the first island in the group. On the beach, I saw a lifeless form. What was that? Was that a person? River? Fortunately, the raven I had hitched a ride with had decided it wanted to investigate, and I flew downward toward the shape lying between some rocks on the beach.

My wings stretched upward and out as I came in for a landing, letting the air slow me down. I landed on a huge uprooted tree on the beach. I eyed the shape between the rocks and hopped off the log to inspect it more closely. It was a dead seal, rotting in the sand. Gross. I tried pulling the raven up and back into the air, but it was definitely more interested in the seal.

I hopped forward and landed atop the corpse; an open wound just inches away. The coppery smell of blood drew the raven's beak downward.

Ugh! I yanked my body out of the raven's. An overwhelming feeling of vertigo came over me for a moment before I felt myself slamming into my own body aboard the boat. I panted and my eyes flew open.

Cassandra's face was inches from mine, her brown eyes sparkling with anticipation. She grabbed my arms. "What happened? Did you find River?"

I sucked in a quick breath. "Cassandra! Let go of me. You're freaking me out."

"Sorry." She stepped back, a look of guilt crossing her freckled face.

Everyone else was looking at me expectantly.

"Well?" Frank asked.

"I couldn't control that bird. He saw a dead seal on the beach, and wanted to have a snack." I shuddered, remembering the smell of blood. "I got the heck out of there when I realized he was going for the all-you-can eat buffet."

Benny wrinkled up his nose. "Nasty."

"Are you going to try again?" Cassandra asked.

My shoulders slumped. "I don't know what good it would do if I can't control where the raven goes."

Ty looked at me sadly. "I thought this was it. I thought we'd find them for sure."

"Don't give up so fast!" Cassandra said animatedly. "Maybe you possessed the wrong raven."

"What?"

"Well, maybe you shouldn't inhabit just *any* raven. Maybe you should have called your totem animal," she said.

I jumped to my feet. "Cassandra, sometimes you can be so *brilliant!*" I hugged her and twirled her around the deck. Her face broke into a grin, and she laughed with delight.

I got myself together and stepped away from her. "Okay, how do I call my totem animal?"

Ty shrugged. "I don't have any drums with me. Maybe since my grandfather already aligned our animals, we can just call them without any kind of ritual."

"I'll give it a try." I closed my eyes and imagined my totem animal, the raven, coming to me. Everything was silent except for the water lapping at the sides of the boat.

Cassandra squealed, and I opened my eyes. A large black bird gripped the railing of the boat and regarded me, tilting its head from one side to the other.

"Thank you," I whispered. I closed my eyes and willed myself to become the bird.

I felt a little pull inside me and suddenly my vantage changed and I was eyeing my friends, staring at me in awe. Ty stepped forward and held onto my body—the one that I was no longer occupying—and made me sit back down on the cushions.

I cawed to my friends, bent my legs, and jumped into the air. Could I control my totem animal better than I could with the last raven? I gave it a try. I looked down at the boat and began to circle over my friends' heads. They stood with their faces tilted up, mouths hanging open. Yes! Now to fly above the islands.

Soaring on a cushion of air, I dipped my wings to the left and to the right, ecstatic to have some control of where I was going and to feel the sensation of flying. I guided my totem animal to the cluster of islands and flew a little closer to the tree line, watching for any sign of humans. I scanned the first island—the one with the dead seal on the beach. A half a dozen gulls were now crowded around the seal, feasting on its remains. I didn't see any sign of people there, even though I circled the small area several times.

The next few islands were clear as well. Finally, I reached the largest of the islands. A weathered cabin was situated in a tiny cove, complete with a dock. I expected there to be a small boat tethered to the dock, but it was empty. Perhaps no one was home. I flew further over the trees. Strange lumpy hills were scattered throughout the island. I could just make them out through the covering of Sitka Spruce and Douglas Firs. They looked to be made of boards and wavy metal planks. What were those?

There! I caught a glimpse of movement near one of the hills. A person? A woman with long dark hair. Thin and weak looking, she crouched beside a berry bush, eating the fruit slowly, as if rationing each one.

I circled overhead and cawed loudly. She was alive! My wings beat hard as I flew over the islands and headed back to the boat. Joy erupted inside of me. I couldn't wait to get back to the boat to tell Ty.

On the return flight, I noticed more clouds rolling in with the wind. These were darker and ominous-looking.

We needed to rescue River and her mom as quickly as possible—before the weather set in. Down below, the boat floated in the choppy iron-gray water. My friends looked up into the sky and pointed.

I landed on the rail and willed myself back into my body. My eyes popped open, and I sucked in a huge breath of air.

"Did you find them?" Ty's hands were on my shoulders; his eyes peering into mine.

"Yes!" I jumped up from the cushions.

"River?" Ty said as he got up to face me.

"Yes! I mean, I don't know. I was above and looking down, and there was someone with long dark hair, and she was crouching down picking berries. She looked very weak and—"

"She's alive!" Ty's face broke into a grin. "I knew it!" He grabbed me and hugged me tightly.

"Where is she?" Detective Coalfield asked. "We'll need to move the boat closer."

I explained that she was on the largest island; the one with lumpy hills scattered about.

"Lumpy hills?" Benny asked.

"Yeah, I don't know what they were, but they almost looked like old collapsed huts. Most of them were about the same size and had grass and ferns growing on top."

Frank furrowed his brows. "Those sound like they could be World War II Quonset huts."

"World War II?" I asked. "Why would they have World War II structures here?"

"Because during the early 1940s, the U.S. was trying to protect the coastlines from invasion," Frank explained. "They had gun batteries and bunkers stationed from Alaska to California."

"Cool," Benny said.

"Well, now we have a starting point for our search," the detective said. He made his way back toward the cabin.

"We need to go over and find Ty's family. Let's start the engine and move over there."

Chapter 31

"If we are all going ashore, we'll have to drop anchor," Frank said.

"Let's do it," the detective said. "We may need everyone on the island to help carry River and her mom if they are injured."

Frank nodded and proceeded to get the anchor in place.

We were in a little cove facing a semi-circular sandy beach—perfect for landing a small boat. There were no visible jagged rocks to catch on the bottom of the vessel.

I stood on the bow while the others climbed off into the inflatable motorized dinghy. Way off in the distance, I saw a speck—a boat perhaps. An uneasy feeling came over me. I made my way back to the dinghy and gingerly climbed aboard.

"I think I see a boat way over there." I squished onto the bench seat next to Ty.

"Probably just somebody out fishing."

"Should someone stay with this boat, just in case?" I asked.

"Nah, it won't take us long to get River and my aunt. We'll be back in no time at all." He put his arm around me and gave my shoulders a squeeze. "Thank you, Jenny. I'll never be able to repay you for finding my family."

I swallowed hard, hoping to shake the strange dark feeling washing over me.

We puttered to shore, and then got out to help pull the dinghy up the beach.

"Why didn't we just anchor by that little cabin I saw on the other side of the island?" Benny grumbled as he shook the water out of his shoes. "There was a dock there."

"Because I spotted the woman on this side of the island. It's a shorter distance to the boat if we have to carry anybody."

"Oh. That makes sense." He shook his leg one more time and a spray of water caught me in the face. "Oops, sorry."

I wiped the water off my cheeks with my sweatshirt.

"Which way should we go?" Cassandra asked.

"This way." I pointed to an area beyond the sand where evergreens grew sparsely.

Ty started running in that direction.

"Whoa!" Frank called to him. "Don't go too fast! Usually, in an area where there are World War II huts and gun batteries, there are holes where the guns were posted. If you go too fast, you may fall in one of them and break your leg."

Ty slowed down just a little and kept his eyes glued to the ground. "Come on, you guys. We've got to find them!"

I caught up to Ty while Cassandra and Benny darted over logs and between bushes on either side of us. I thought about their totem animals. Would my friends be this sure on their feet without their animal guides? Detective Coalfield and Frank followed behind, keeping a protective eye on our group.

I halted abruptly, losing faith in my ability to find the girl with the long dark hair.

Ty stared at me. "What's wrong? Why'd you stop?"

Shaking my head, I glanced in all directions. The trees were dense here and I felt disoriented. I could still hear the ocean off in the distance, but we were on an island, so it didn't give me any reference to our location. "I've lost my sense of direction in the woods. I don't know which way to go."

Benny and Cassandra bounded up to us. "What's the matter?" Cassandra asked.

"It was easy to know where to go from the air," I said. "But now…"

"Totem animals," Benny whispered.

"What?" I asked.

"They'll help us. Let's call them."

We stood in a circle while Frank and the detective caught up to us. Closing our eyes, we imagined our animals coming to the rescue. Sure enough they appeared, not in the white vapor form they did on the night Henry was with us, but in solid form. They were so real, if I hadn't known what each person's totem animal was, I would've run screaming through the trees.

Detective Coalfield's hand dropped to the gun in the holster at his side. Frank grabbed the man's arm and nodded toward the bear, then pointed to himself.

Benny's eyebrows shot upward as he watched his rabbit sniffing the air, his nose twitching rapidly. Cassandra's deer took one glance back at us, and then both the rabbit and the deer darted ahead, showing us the way. As we ran to keep up, both my raven and Ty's raven flew ahead, occasionally lighting onto a branch to wait for our arrival. Frank's bear lumbered along beside us, and I caught a glimpse of Detective Coalfield's eagle as it soared over the treetops.

All of a sudden, the forest thinned out, and the animals stopped their mad dash. We slowed down to a walk as we reached the area where the Quonset huts stood.

Ty stepped forward, his eyes seemed to scan the area, taking in everything. Walking slowly ahead, he knelt down to examine the ground. "Footprints," he whispered, pointing to the impression in the dirt.

The print was on the small side; definitely not a man's shoe.

He stood up and was still. Aside from the sound of the ocean, there was no other sound. No birds, no insects. Just silence.

A rustling noise made everyone jump. Ty's head whipped around, looking for its source. There it was again. He sprinted toward the noise with the rest of us in hot pursuit. The bushes scraped against our legs as we flew by. We ran past the first Quonset hut and tore through the brush to the next one.

There, lying beside a huckleberry bush, was a frail woman with long dark hair. She was wearing tattered jeans, a flannel shirt several sizes too big, and an enormous canvas jacket. Her cheeks were sunken in from hunger, and her brown eyes barely had any life left in them.

"River!" Ty shouted.

The woman turned her face up to Ty's, clearly startled, but too weak to react. "Ty?" she muttered. "I must be dreaming. Maybe I'm dead."

"Aunt Cathy?" Ty dropped to the ground beside her. "Oh my God!"

My eyes quickly scanned her body. I noticed where the jeans had ripped and exposed her legs, and her skin underneath was charred and oozing. She must have been burned in the explosion. It looked infected.

"Ty," I whispered. I knelt down next to him and pointed to her legs.

His eyes skimmed her injuries and then met mine.

"You have to help her." I grabbed his hand and placed it on one of her legs.

"But, what about River?" He glanced at me, and then turned to the woman. "Aunt Cathy, is River here?"

She nodded.

"Where?" He removed his hands from her body.

"Ty..."

His aunt tried sitting up and fell back on her elbows, wincing. Frank went around behind her, kneeled down, and gently lifted her upper body onto his lap, cradling her. She pointed to one of the Quonset Huts.

"She's here!" Ty jumped up and started to run to the hut.

"Wait!" Aunt Cathy struggled to form the words. "Ty, please... you don't understand."

He turned to look at her. "But I have to go get her!"

She shook her head sadly. "River is..."

"No!" He raced to the hut. I scrambled up from the ground and ran after him, dread filling my heart. I reached him quickly and tried to pull him back from the shack.

Wrenching his arm away from me, he took a step forward. The hut was not much bigger than a broom closet and was partially caved in. There, just inside the doorway, dark hair peeked out from under a blanket of cut sword ferns, which had been laid on top. Flies buzzed around inside the small enclosed area, and the sweet, sickening smell of death hung in the air.

A low, wounded-animal sound escaped Ty's lips.

"Ty." I tried to pull him away, but he struggled to stand firm. "Come on," I pleaded. "Let's leave her be."

He sank to his knees, moaning. "River, no, no, no, no. Oh please, God, no!" Then the sobs came, wracking his body.

I turned around to look at the others, who were standing silently, their faces white with shock. Kneeling down beside him, I rubbed his back. "I'm so sorry, Ty. I'm so sorry." I let him cry for what seemed like hours, but was probably only a few minutes.

"Hey," I whispered to him. "I know how hard this is— but you've got to think about your aunt now. She's in really bad shape, and she needs your help."

Closing his eyes, his sobs subsided. He took a deep breath, and wiped his eyes. "I know, I know—you're right."

I stood up and waited for him to come to terms with River's death. Another few moments went by, and finally he stood up, his face contorted with grief. My heart broke in two watching him suffer. Gently, I put my arm around his waist and led him to his aunt, who was still lying on the ground, cradled by Frank.

Tears streamed down her cheeks as she looked up at Ty.

"I couldn't save her." She covered her face with her hands.

Ty sank down to the ground next to her. He took a deep breath, let it out slowly, and wiped his face on his t-shirt sleeve.

"Let's see your leg, Aunty." He sniffled, and then pulled the tattered denim fabric away from her skin. Looking alarmed, he let the fabric fall back over the infected area. "This is not good. We've got to get her to the hospital."

"Wait," I interjected. "Try to do your healing on her. If you can help her even a little bit, she'll be better off for the boat ride home."

Ty nodded and placed his hands over her legs and closed his eyes. Nothing happened.

I touched his shoulder. "You have to focus."

Then, suddenly I felt a surge of energy in the air. I could almost see the warmth glowing around his fingers. Cathy sighed and leaned back onto Frank's lap.

"While Ty works his magic, do you mind if I ask you some questions?" Detective Coalfield said as he knelt down beside the woman. "I mean, if you are feeling up to it."

"I don't mind," she whispered hoarsely.

"First of all, was the boat explosion an accident?"

216

Cathy shook her head.

"Did your husband do this?"

She nodded and wiped the tears from her cheeks.

"I'll kill him," Ty muttered.

Gently, I redirected his hands to his aunt's injuries.

"Where did you get these clothes?" the detective asked.

I took in her outfit. Her tattered jeans were definitely hers, but the flannel shirt and canvas jacket obviously belonged to a man.

"The boy," she said weakly.

"The boy?" Frank's demeanor changed almost immediately to watchful and alert.

"Yes." Her voice cracked a little. "The little boy. His father lives in that cabin on the other side of the island. Mean man." Cathy coughed, her throat obviously dry.

Benny rummaged through the backpack that Detective Coalfield had slung on the ground, and took out a bottle of water. He opened it and handed it to Cathy. She accepted the water gratefully and drank nearly half the bottle in one gulp.

"Whoa, slow down." Frank took the bottle away. "Don't drink it too fast—it can make you sick." He gave it back to her and watched her take small sips.

"The boy brought you the clothes?" Detective Coalfield asked gently. "Where is he now?"

"He's trying to get help... and to get away from his father." She took another sip of the water.

"How is he going to do that?" Cassandra asked.

Cathy shook her head. "I told him not to, but he was determined. He's sure to drown—please, help him."

Frank cleared his throat. "Don't worry, we'll find him. You don't happen to know the boy's name do you?"

"Devon."

Flash.

I dragged my raft to the water's edge and put it in.

The waves pulled it away from me.
Splash! There, I got on.
Hey, there's a boat over there.
Maybe it's okay. It's not my dad's boat.
But there's another one coming.
If I get close enough, they'll see me.
They'll rescue me and take me home.

"The raft! Devon built a raft and he's putting it into the water."

"Devon's here?" the detective asked, looking stunned.

"How did you know that?" Cathy asked me.

"She's psychic," Ty answered.

Cathy looked puzzled, and then she seemed to understand. "Is that how you found me?"

"I guess so," he said. "But we couldn't have done it without Grandfather's help."

"Do you know where Devon took his raft?" Detective Coalfield raked his hands through his short hair.

The frail woman pointed in the direction we came. "To the cove with the sandy beach."

"We just came from there!" Cassandra said. "We must have just missed him."

"Hurry," the detective said. "Let's get her to our boat and get Devon."

"I hope it's not too late," Benny said, frowning.

Chapter 32

Carefully, the detective picked Cathy up and carried her through the forest. We walked in a group, watching out for any holes or obstacles he might step into.

When we finally reached the shore, we immediately noticed a boat approaching, maybe no more than a mile away.

"What is that?" Benny squinted at the vessel. "It looks like they are checking us out."

Helping Frank and Cassandra carry the dinghy back into the water, I briefly glanced at the oncoming boat. "Let's worry about getting her back to safety for now."

Cathy moaned as Detective Coalfield, Frank, and Ty situated her into the dinghy, now bobbing in shallow water. They propped her up in Ty's arms, and pushed it further out until they could both climb in.

"Jenny, you and the others stay here and see if you can spot Devon," the detective said. "We need to get her onboard." The rubber boat's engine sputtered to life and they took off, leaving us on shore.

"You guys go that way, I'll check on this side of the beach." I ran to the left, where an outcropping of rocks stood. Maybe I could get a better view of the water from higher up. I scaled the rocks and stood on the highest point. I looked out to the right and saw my friends searching the water. So far, nothing.

Scanning the water to the left, I looked for anything out of the ordinary. I noticed the boat I had seen earlier approaching the island. It was getting much closer, and the occupants seemed very interested in what Ty, Detective Coalfield, and Frank were doing.

A shout rang out from the right side of the beach. My head whipped around. Benny and Cassandra had spotted something in the water, about a hundred yards out. I clambered over the rocks and nearly lost my footing. I jumped to the last rock before hitting the sand, my feet leaving deep footprints where I landed.

Benny and Cassandra waded into the water, waving their arms and shouting for help. The iron-gray water was choppy, and the wind had really picked up. I splashed into the water and came up alongside Benny. "What's going on?"

He pointed to a blob of wood debris and a dark head of hair bobbing above the waves. A little boy was flailing in the water.

"He's drowning!" I screamed.

Cassandra's face was pale. "I'm not much of a swimmer. If I swam out there, I'd probably drown right along with him."

"How 'bout you, Benny?" I asked. "Can you swim?"

He nodded. "Let's go get him together."

"Hurry," I shouted as we waded in deeper. "I don't think he can hang on much longer." While Benny and I swam out to Devon, Cassandra shouted to the detective and Frank. "We found Devon! Help!"

Frank had just pulled Cathy onto the big boat. I heard him say to Ty, "Stay here, I'm going to get the kids." He jumped back into the dinghy and motored through the water as fast as the vessel could go.

A few yards ahead of us in the ocean, Devon floundered, waving his arms. His head disappeared into the spray several times, before resurfacing again. Panic clouded his features as he struggled to stay above the waves. Around him, fragments of the raft floated—the logs that he had tied together were barely two inches in diameter, and wouldn't even have held a cat, let alone a five or six year old boy. The raft had completely fallen apart and wasn't even solid enough for him to grab onto and use as a float board.

I used my best crawl stroke to get to him as fast as I could. Benny was slightly behind me. When I reached the boy, he grabbed onto me and climbed up me, like a little monkey. His hands pushed down on my head, making me go under water. Struggling to get a breath of air, I tried to pull him off my neck; he was choking me. Benny reached him just in time and pulled him off me.

"Devon," he said sharply. "Calm down—or you'll pull Jenny down with you."

The boy's eyes were opened wide and his face was white, looking like a wild animal. I knew at this point he couldn't be reasoned with—he was in full survival mode.

Frank pulled up alongside us in the dinghy. He pulled Devon into the boat first, then Benny and me.

"Thank God!" I sat dripping on the bench seat.

Benny gathered Devon up, shivering, and cradled him like a baby. "It's going to be all right."

I looked over to the big boat and noticed the other boat had come much closer to it. A man stood on deck with binoculars—he was focused on Ty and Cathy. Ty had carried his aunt into the large cabin, and the binoculars followed them. That was odd. Wouldn't he be more focused on the rescue effort of the drowning boy? Why wouldn't he come over here and see if he could help us?

Another motor sound buzzed around the corner. I craned my neck to see who else was approaching.

221

Suddenly, a smaller boat was visible. It raced to the cove we were anchored in.

Flash.

That little brat!

Who are those people?

I've got to get Devon away from them.

They won't take him!

Over my dead body!

"Detective!" I called out over the water. "Pull the anchor! It's Vince McLeod—Devon's dad!"

He looked up at the approaching boat and then back at us. Scrambling to the back of the deck, he tried getting the anchor up. He looked frustrated after a moment. "I don't know what I'm doing! I think this thing is automatic but I can't find the controls."

"Hurry, Frank!" I shouted.

"Hey!" A voice sounded from the beach.

"Oh my God. We forgot about Cassandra." Benny paled.

Cassandra stood on shore waving her arms. Frank aimed for the beach. "You're going to have to swim just a little," he called out to her. "I don't want to catch the bottom on the rocks; it's too shallow."

Wading into the water, looking horror-stricken, Cassandra started toward us. The water hit the bottom of her chin and she took in a mouthful of it. Spluttering, she reached her hands above the waves, undoubtedly standing on her tip-toes.

"Come on, Cassandra! Swim!" I leaned over the rubber wall of the dinghy and reached my hands out to her. "I'll pull you in."

Another wave came and knocked Cassandra off her feet. Her head went under.

Frank reached under his bench seat and pulled out a life jacket. A coil of rope lay on the bottom of the boat and he looped one end through the arm hole in the jacket. "Toss her this," he said, handing it to me.

I made sure Frank had one end of the rope before I threw the jacket out as far as I could. Too far. It sailed past Cassandra's head.

The sound of a gunshot pierced the air.

"Jesus! They're shooting at us!" Benny yelped.

"Get down," ordered Frank, as he shoved Benny and Devon to the bottom of the inflatable craft.

I kept my head down as low as I could while I pulled in the rope, hand over hand. Popping my body up for a moment, I carefully aimed and threw the life jacket at Cassandra. It landed with a splat, just inches from her nose.

More gunfire rang out. I glanced sideways and saw Detective Coalfield on the deck of the larger boat, shooting back at Devon's father. Ty emerged from the cabin, eyes huge. "Get back in there!" the Detective shouted at him. "Call the Coast Guard!"

"Grab it!" I yelled at Cassandra. She went under again as a large wave rolled over her. She hadn't come back up. I waited a moment longer, weighing my options. Either I jumped in after her or we left her behind to save the rest of us. No, that wasn't an option at all. I stood up, ready to dive in.

A bullet whizzed past my ear.

"Get down!" Frank shouted.

"But..."

"You'll be shot," he said sternly.

I looked back to where Cassandra had gone down. No, I couldn't let her drown. Just as I readied myself to jump in, her head bobbed above the waves and she spluttered water out of her nose and mouth. "Grab the life jacket! It's right in front of you!"

Cassandra reached for the vest as a bullet thudded into the side of the dinghy. A hiss of air whooshed out.

"Grab it!" I yelled. Her fingertips brushed the fabric and then with one push forward, she grasped it. Pulling on the rope with all my might, I tried to stay low while bullets peppered the water around us.

Frank and I leaned over and pulled Cassandra in with a thud. The rubber boat sank lower into the water and more air hissed out of the side.

Devon's dad fired another shot, but his gun must have been out of bullets. His enraged roar sailed over the water. He pulled out a box of ammo and began reloading his pistol. We saw our opportunity to make it to the larger vessel.

"Hold on," Frank said. We accelerated toward our boat. Salty spray hit my face as the rubber boat skipped across the choppy waves, leaking air with each bump.

Bang! Another hole was blown into the side of it. The man had been quick to reload. Devon shrieked; his eyes filled with terror. "No, Dad! Don't shoot!"

Benny leaned over, pushing Cassandra and Devon further to the boat's bottom, covering their bodies with his.

Seconds later, we pulled alongside the vessel. Detective Coalfield grabbed the rope that Frank tossed to him and clipped the cables from the boat onto the metal rings on the half-inflated dinghy. The older man handed Devon up to the detective and then Cassandra, Benny, and I quickly climbed out of the smaller boat. Frank jumped up onto the deck and went into the cabin to start the engine, and Detective Coalfield started the automatic winch to secure the dinghy to the boat.

"You guys get in the cabin," he ordered, drawing his gun. "And stay low."

"What about the anchor?" I asked.

"Frank's taking care of it."

The engine started. Frank and Ty were working together on getting the boat dislodged from the bottom, winging it in a circle. The anchor came loose and the automatic winch started reeling in the cable. The dinghy was in place too, even though it looked more like a kiddie pool that had seen one too many summers. We should've just left it behind.

On the other side of us, the other boat was approaching slowly. The man with the binoculars had a gun too.

Chapter 33

"What do you want from us?" Detective Coalfield bellowed.

"You know what I want." The man's voice carried over the water.

Flash.

"Are you sure you want to go through with this?" the lady with the Louis Vuitton handbag asked. "You could just divorce her..."

"But then we wouldn't get the life insurance money. You do want to continue to live like this, right?" he asked, pointing to her jewelry.

She nodded, and slowly a wide grin spread across her face. "Can I get those earrings from Tiffany's I've been wanting?"

"It's Tom Lisyansky, Cathy's husband," I said to the detective. "He did this for the insurance money."

Frank peered out at us through the cabin windows. "Should I get us out of here?" His muffled voice sounded through the glass.

"Hand her over!" the man shouted.

"Stall," I whispered. I needed to do something.

On the other side of us, Vince McLeod had his gun pointed at us. He was only about fifty yards away. The wind had picked up even more, and his dark hair blew around his eyes, making him look wilder and more desperate.

"I told her!" Vince yelled. "I told her she shouldn't leave me. But she wouldn't listen!"

What was he talking about?

"She said I was unstable! Me!" He laughed and ran his fingers through his windblown hair. "Not once did she look in the mirror. If she had, she would've realized that it was all *her*."

My eyes darted to the detective and then to Cassandra and Benny. Ty quietly came out of the cabin, his body still—focused like a cat.

"Get in there," the detective said, pointing to the cabin, his face stony. "All of you."

"Stop!" Lisyansky shouted.

"Stop!" Vince McLeod yelled at the same time. "Don't go anywhere, any of you! You can't take my son."

Benny grabbed my hand and gave me a meaningful look. He wanted me to do something. "Totem animals, ancient spirits, anybody," he hissed. "We've got to call on them again."

I glanced at Ty, who had overheard Benny. He nodded at me.

We inched together and joined hands, closing our eyes. Ty began chanting something in Tlingit. I focused on my totem animal. And then it occurred to me that I should also try to talk to the Native American from Ketchikan. I didn't even know his name, but I pictured him just the way I saw him on the boardwalk, wearing his ceremonial robe.

We need help. Please—call the ancient Tlingit warriors and all the tribes from this area. Protect us and keep us safe. Then, without missing a beat, I called upon God and the angels to come and help. I bit my lip, concentrating so hard, I barely heard the shouts around me.

"Jenny!" Ty shook my shoulder. "Look!"

I opened my eyes and my mouth dropped open. Around us, everywhere, were Tlingits in warrior clothing, totem animals, and angels. They swirled around us and the boats in a vortex of white haze.

The cabin door burst open and Devon appeared on deck with us. He was small and scared. But I sensed an internal strength in this boy.

"Devon, go back inside," I said. "It's not safe here."

Turning to his father's boat, he yelled, "Dad! Leave me alone! I want to be with Mommy!"

His father's face contorted with rage. "If I can't have you, nobody can." Raising his gun, he took aim and squeezed the trigger.

Cassandra screamed. Benny flung himself in front of Devon, protecting his body from the oncoming bullet. Before I even had time to react, I felt feathers brush my arm. I stared at the bullet as it hung in mid-air before landing on the deck with a clink. Glancing over my shoulder, the form of an angel hovered above Devon and then flew out between Lisyansky's boat and ours.

Ty's uncle took aim at his nephew and fired a shot. Out of nowhere, another being appeared beside the angel. A beautiful girl with long hair... River. She stood fiercely beside the angelic creature and blocked the bullet. Ty gasped and reached out to her. For an instant, her demeanor softened, and she turned back to look at us. Then, she was back in the battle. Apparently, Lisyansky couldn't see the angel or River. He was astounded to see his bullet drop out of the air and into the water.

"What the hell?" Detective Coalfield looked around us. "I swear I'm seeing white shapes. Are those angels or animals?"

Both men opened fire on us, the shots so loud the sound pierced my ear drums. The group of us hit the deck with our hands over our heads. I peeked out over my arm as totem animals, Native Americans in battle gear, and angels warded off each bullet. Ty was completely focused on River as she helped to protect us.

Detective Coalfield got up into a crouch and shouted. "Frank! Get us out of here!"

Our boat surged forward, shots still flying. Devon's dad and Lisyansky scrambled to their controls and started their engines, and proceeded to chase after us.

"Come on!" the detective shouted over the noise. "Get into the cabin!"

We tripped over ourselves trying to fit through the cabin door all at once. Ty grabbed my arm. "Stay low." He pushed down on my back so that we were squatting. The boat rode up and down in the choppy waves. I grabbed the edge of the dining seats to regain my balance.

"Where's your aunt?" I got down on my hands and knees and started crawling closer to where Frank was steering the boat, and stood up beside the wheel.

"I carried her to one of the bedrooms and laid her on the floor. She would be in danger of getting shot if she were up on the bed."

"I'll go check on her," Cassandra said, crawling toward the sleeping quarters.

"What about Devon?" I asked.

"I've got him," Benny wrapped the little boy in his arms and sat on the teak floor.

Detective Coalfield burst through the door, crouched down low, and crab-crawled over to Frank. "Gun it!" he ordered the older man.

"I'm at full throttle," he said.

"What about the Coast Guard?" I asked with clenched teeth as the boat's speed threatened to knock me off my feet.

"On their way," Frank answered.

"Jenny, you need to get down," the detective said.

"I just want to check one thing." I looked out at the stormy sky. Our spirit allies were still with us, shielding us from harm. A stray bullet got through their defenses and thwacked into the wood frame of the window.

Ty yanked me down. "You've got to get low."

But as we sped through the rough water, the sound of bullets nearing our boat was diminishing. In the distance, I could hear the syncopated hum of a helicopter approaching.

My muscles were aching as I crouched down beside Ty. The anxious feeling in my chest bubbled up through me. I had to get up and see what was happening.

"I'm going out there." I got up and bounced my way toward the door of the cabin.

"Jenny, no!" Ty jumped up after me.

I yanked the door open. The salty mist coated my skin and the wind whipped at my hair. Without thinking it through, I walked across the deck. The surface rebounded up and down under my feet, and I nearly lost my balance. Reaching for the rails to steady myself, I looked back at our wake.

Lisyansky's boat was to the left, and he was speeding up. If Frank couldn't get us going faster, we would be in trouble soon. McLeod was to the right, lagging behind a little further in his smaller boat. But he was also gaining a little more speed. Both men had their guns drawn. What would happen if they both caught up to us?

"Jenny, what the hell—" Ty tried to pull me back.

Lisyansky held on to his steering wheel with one hand and pointed his pistol at us with the other. He squeezed off a round. The bullets rained out, but none of them even came close to us.

I stood frozen as hundreds of Tlingit spirits swooped around Ty's uncle. He flinched. Unseen hands wrenched the gun from his grasp. It flew up into the air and skittered across his deck.

A Coast Guard helicopter flew toward us and hovered over the boats chasing us.

"Put down your weapons!" A voice boomed through a loudspeaker.

In one boat, Lisyansky cowered as the helicopter beat the air above him. He glanced at Ty, and then crouched down and scooted across the deck. Picking his gun up, he pointed at the helicopter. "Get out of here!" he shouted. "Or I'll shoot!"

McLeod saw his opportunity to fire at us. A group of angels and Indian spirits surrounded the man. He pointed his weapon at us, but the band of spirits pulled his arm away. The gun went off, the sound of it completely lost in the chopping of the helicopter blades.

A scream rang out over the noise. Lisyansky flew backward, a dark stain spreading across his blue shirt. McLeod's bullet had ricocheted off his boat's metal railing and struck Lisyansky in the gut. McLeod's face registered shock as he stared at the blood staining the other man's shirt.

McLeod watched Ty's uncle fall and looked at his gun in surprise. His boat hit a big wave and suddenly he thudded to the deck. A second wave rocked the vessel, and he flopped over the low railing of his boat and splashed into the angry water.

What had just happened? We weren't sure what we had witnessed. Ty wrapped his arms around me. The wind from the helicopter lashed at our hair. The cold had seeped into my bones, but the warmth from Ty took the chill away.

We looked back at the scene behind us. Now that the two boats were unmanned, they sped off in opposite directions.

Detective Coalfield threw open the door. "What the hell are you two doing out here?" His face was red and worry furrowed his brow. "I told you, it's not safe!"

"It's over," I said, still holding onto Ty.

"Over?" The detective stepped out onto the deck. The helicopter still hovered above, probably uncertain as to which boat to chase.

"Stay close by," the voice boomed over the loudspeaker. "Help is on the way."

Frank, who had been communicating with the Coast Guard, steered the vessel away from the helicopter and back toward where we had come in. Soon, Benny, Cassandra, and Devon joined us on deck. Frank cut the engine and stepped out of the cabin as well. We watched as the Coast Guard helicopter sent a rescuer down into the water to pull Devon's dad out. He wasn't moving. I couldn't tell if he had survived or not.

I kneeled down beside Devon and put my arm around him. "Are you okay, buddy?"

His big brown eyes filled with tears, and he nodded solemnly. "I just want to go home and see my mommy."

I looked up at Frank, whose expression had changed from man-in-charge to softie. He kneeled down on Devon's other side. "What's your mommy's name?"

"Louise."

"Louise? I have a daughter named Louise." Frank was looking at Devon with awe.

Flash.

A much younger Frank wearing a uniform stepped out of the car.

"Daddy!"

A little girl with wavy brown hair ran to him. He crouched down and she threw her arms around his neck.

"How's my big girl?"

"Fine, Daddy! Did you bring me something?"

He laughed and pulled the bag off his shoulder. Unzipping the top, he drew out a doll with wavy brown hair.

The little girl shrieked with delight. "She looks just like me!"

"Yes, she does."
She turned her dark eyes to his, smiled, and gave him a kiss on the cheek.
"Thank you, Daddy! I love her—and I love you."
"I love you too, Louise."
I took in a sharp breath. "Frank! Could this be—"
"My grandson." His voice choked with emotion. "Yes, I do believe he is."

Chapter 34

Another chopper loomed on the horizon. The white and red helicopter arrived quickly and hovered a safe distance away from our boat.

"Okay," Detective Coalfield said. "Let's go get Cathy." He, Frank, and Ty went back into the boat and emerged a few minutes later.

"Careful with her." Ty held the door open so Frank wouldn't bump her head against it when he carried her out to the deck.

The detective gave a thumbs up to the pilot, and the aircraft moved into position directly over our boat. The wind beat furiously against the water. I squinted as the salty spray clung to my eyelashes.

A gurney was lowered out the hatch, along with a Coast Guard medic. With the aid of Frank and Detective Coalfield, the rescuer strapped Ty's aunt to the gurney.

"Can I go with her?" Ty shouted over the noise.

"Are you family?" The man cinched the last strap and gave it a tug.

"Yeah, she's my aunt."

The man nodded. "I'll be back to get you after she's in."

"Okay, we're ready," the man said into the radio clipped to his survival suit.

Ty looked up, worry creasing his face.

As they rose into the air, I gripped his arm. "She'll be all right."

"God, I hope so."

He turned back to me. "Listen, Jenny... it may be a while before I see you again." Swallowing hard, he pulled me to him. "I know you'll be leaving in a week or so. But I just wanted you to know how much it meant to have you here."

I looked into his eyes and gave a little nod.

"You..." his voice broke. Wiping a tear from his face, he went on. "You found River."

I waited while he regained composure.

"Thank you. We saw her today... her energy lives on." His eyes misted over again.

"Without you, I would still be wondering what happened to her. That would be hell."

Hugging him tightly, I whispered into his ear, "I'm sorry about your cousin." I pulled away from him and held his face in my hands. "She was so lucky to have you as family. A part of her will always exist right here." I laid my hand on his chest. He pulled me in and hugged me so hard I thought I wouldn't be able to breathe.

The rescuer was slowly lowered back onto the boat.

"You'd better go." I drew his face to mine and kissed him gently. "I'll visit you and Cathy in the hospital."

He kissed me back and joined the Coast Guard man. After they were both secured in the harnesses, the helicopter crew pulled them up, and they flew away from the boat.

I watched as the aircraft became a small dot on the horizon.

My shoulders slumped, and I felt like all the energy had drained out of me. A sob escaped me and I covered my face. The adrenaline rush had ended, and the dam holding my feelings in place let loose, spilling them in a torrent of emotions. Horror, sorrow, and anger surged through me. Why did people do such horrible things? I fervently hoped that Tom Lisyansky, and Devon's father, were dead. Greed and jealousy were indeed powerful demons. But then guilt set in. No, I would not wish them dead. I had to be careful not to let anger get the best of me. It was not for me to decide what would happen to them.

"Are you cold?" Benny took off his hoodie and wrapped it around my shoulders.

"Thanks, Benny."

"It'll be okay," he said. "It'll be okay."

After being strong for Ty and trying to reassure him that things would be okay, it was nice to have someone do the same for me.

Chapter 35

I hated the beeping sound of the heart monitor. It reminded me too much of the time I had spent in the hospital. This time, though, it was Ty's aunt who was hooked up to the machines. An IV drip ran from the hanging bag to the line in Cathy's arm.

My thoughts ran wild. What would I say to Ty? I was leaving in a few days.

"Thank you for sitting with me." Ty's voice jarred me out of my head. He reached across his sleeping aunt and squeezed my hand.

"You're welcome. How is she?"

He shrugged. "The doctors said she should be okay. She was really dehydrated, and she has lost too much weight. She'll probably be here for another few days at least."

"What about the infection in her legs?"

"That's healing nicely. The doctors couldn't figure out why the infection hadn't spread." He smiled and looked embarrassed.

I thought of the way he had put his hands on Cathy's wounds after we had discovered that River had died. It was a miracle that he had the power to heal.

"Are you coming for the last day of Fine Arts Camp?" I tucked my hair behind my ears and fidgeted with my earrings.

He shook his head. "I need to stay with my aunt. Mom and I are taking turns sitting with her."

"I understand, of course. Will I see you again? We leave on Saturday morning." I bit my lip, knowing what the answer would be.

He picked up his chair and moved it next to mine. He took my hand in his. "Jenny—I am so grateful you're here with me." He swallowed hard. "God, I hate this. But..."

"But you need to focus on your family." I glanced at Cathy, who murmured something in her sleep.

"It's just that I feel like they need my undivided attention right now. And when I'm with you, I can't focus on anything else." His brown eyes met mine. "I would forget everything and get lost in you."

I reached up and traced the outline of his face. Pulling him closer to me, I kissed his lips gently. "I know, Ty. It's okay."

"This really sucks. If it were any other circumstance, I wouldn't let you go. I've fallen so hard for you."

"You don't have to explain. I fell for you too."

He looked pained, and raked his hand through his hair. "Can we at least keep in touch? Maybe after all this is over and things have settled down..."

I nodded. "I'll miss you. Take care of your family."

Rising from my chair, I walked to the door and looked back.

"Jenny. Wait."

I stopped, wondering if he had changed his mind.

"I almost forgot." He stood up, dug in his jeans pocket, and pulled something out. The light from the window glinted in his hand and a dancing shaft of light illuminated the ceiling. Ty held out his hand toward me. In his palm, a beautiful silver bracelet caught the light. "My grandfather wanted you to have this."

I crossed the room toward him and took the slim, beautifully carved bracelet out of his hand. The head of the raven curved in toward one end, while the tail feathers curved in toward the other. It was open in the middle. I bent it slightly and slipped it onto my wrist. I held my arm out and noticed the intricate Tlingit design carved around it.

"Oh," I whispered. "I can't accept this. It's too expensive."

Ty shook his head. "You have to. It's a gift from Grandfather. It's a thank you—it would insult him if you refused it. Besides, it's a raven. Our totem animal."

I touched the metal. A warmth spread through my fingers, and I knew it belonged to me.

"Thank you. Please tell him that I love it."

He nodded. Our eyes met again. Finally, he stepped back and sat back in his chair next to his aunt.

I made my way to the door again. Ty was special. Deep down, I was disturbed that I didn't run back to him. I could have said that I would wait for him—could have told him that someday we could be together. But I held back. I took one last look back at him.

There was something so noble and yet so sad about his face. I fought the urge to return to his side. But I knew if I did, I might not be able to leave.

Chapter 36

The sound of the jet filled my ears as it flew overhead.

"Oh, that's loud."

"Just like you." Jackson smirked at me.

"You're goofy, kid." I cuffed him lightly on the side of the head.

"Ow!"

I rolled my eyes and hoisted my luggage onto the scale.

"Okay, you're all set." The lady at the Alaska Airlines counter smiled at me. "May I help who's next?"

"We still have at least a half hour before we board." Dad stepped away from the line of people waiting to check in. "Feel like having some pie at The Nugget?"

"Definitely." I grinned. "I'm so glad it's just down the hall. I can't go without having another slice of pie."

"Jenny!"

The sliding doors to the tiny airport burst open. I turned to see Cassandra flying toward us. She threw her arms around me and nearly bowled me over.

"You cannot leave without saying goodbye!"

I untangled myself from her. "I thought we already said goodbye when we packed our stuff up in the dorm room. Remember?"

Cassandra wrinkled up her nose. "But that wasn't a *proper* goodbye. Proper goodbyes happen before a ship sails or at places like the airport. Hey! Like that scene at the end of that old movie, Casablanca, when Bogart says to Bergman, "I think this is the beginning of a beautiful friendship.""

I shook my head. "No, no, you've got it mixed up. That was the line that Bogart said to Louie. What he said to Bergman was, 'We'll always have Paris.' And later he says, 'Here's looking at you, kid.'"

"Oh, whatever." Cassandra smiled at me and giggled. "I do think this is the beginning of a beautiful friendship, though, don't you?"

Laughing, I hugged her tightly. "Yes. Care to have some pie with us?"

"Peanut butter?"

"Yup."

"Then absolutely!"

Cassandra and I sat at a small table while the rest of my family occupied a larger one. She picked up her fork and took a huge bite. "Ohmyga." Her cheeks bulged out like a hamster carrying a winter's supply of seeds.

"I know, right?" I took a bite and savored the creamy peanut butter. This was just one of the many things I would miss about Sitka.

She finished chewing and swallowed. "Hey, where are Benny, Frank, and Detective Coalfield?"

"They left a couple of days ago."

"But they didn't say goodbye!"

"Yeah, they did. They came to the last Fine Arts Camp performance, remember?"

"But that wasn't…"

"I know. It wasn't a proper goodbye." I winked at her. "That just means you'll have to come to Seattle for a visit."

Her eyes widened. "Are you inviting me down for a visit?"

"I would love that."

She let her fork fall to her plate and fist-bumped me. "That would be awesome!"

Inhaling the rest of her pie in mere seconds, her face took on a quizzical look. "So, I've been thinking…why do you think Tom Lisyansky came back to the area where he killed his daughter and tried killing his wife?"

"I actually asked the detective that myself." I pushed a piece of pie crust around on my plate. "He said that oftentimes, criminals return to the scene of the crime—just like you see in those TV shows."

"Huh." She licked her fork. "Do they get some kind of sick pleasure out of visiting the murder scene?"

"I guess so. And he might have come back to see that he hadn't left behind any evidence. But with Lisyansky, we'll never really know what drove him to go back there. He pretty much died instantly after the bullet hit him."

"At least Devon's dad lived," Cassandra said. "I bet he'll be in jail for a very long time."

"And Frank's got his daughter back—and a grandson to boot."

"Sometimes, there really are happy endings." She caught the eye of the waitress and called her over. "May I have another piece of pie, please? Peach this time?"

The waitress smiled. "Sure, hon. I'll be right back with that. How 'bout you?"

"No, thanks, I'm fine." My phone buzzed in my pocket. I glanced at the screen. A text message—it was from Mike.

My brows furrowed as I read.

"Jenny, I can't stand this anymore. Please call me."

Chapter 37

The wheels touched down on the runway, jerking me to the right. Rocky landing. Jackson pushed my arm away from his.

"Watch it!" He scowled at me.

"Dude, it's not my fault the pilot's having an off day."

He stood up and stuffed his sweatshirt into his backpack.

"Jackson, sit down!" Mom said sharply. "You're not supposed to get up until we reach the gate, and they've turned the 'fasten your seatbelt' sign off."

"Ugh!" He plopped back down and squirmed in his seat.

"Buckle up," I hissed as the stewardess approached us.

He glared at me and snapped the clasp together.

Ignoring him, I got out my cell phone and texted my friends.

"You're back!" Julia texted.

"Yup. I have lots to tell you guys."

"Juicy details?"

"Sort of."

We reached the gate, and all the passengers crowded into the aisle.

My phone buzzed again. Mike.

"Jenny. I feel really bad about this. Can we talk?" His message blinked up at me.

I hesitated, and stared at my screen. The rows cleared out. I texted back. "Maybe."

The cleaning crew boarded the plane and started going through the aisles methodically. My mom waited at the exit. "Jenny, come on!"

Slinging my backpack on my shoulder, I walked to the front.

"What took you so long?" she asked.

"Uh, just texting someone."

She gave me a knowing look. I had almost forgotten that she was a little psychic herself.

We walked through the enclosed gate, the air conditioning of the airplane giving way to the heat of the late summer day.

"What baggage carousel did they announce?" The heaviness of my pack dug into my shoulder.

"2A," Mom answered.

Jackson and Dad had already disappeared in the throng of travelers.

The walk to the escalator seemed to take forever. My bag felt twenty pounds heavier than it had when I had first gotten off the plane. Mom stepped onto the escalator and I was right behind her. Jackson and Dad were already there, and had just pulled one of our bags off the carousel.

"Jenny!"

"Did you call me, Dad? I'm right here." I set my backpack down next to Mom.

"Huh?" He pulled another bag off the rotating platform. "I didn't call you."

"Jenny! Over here!"

I turned around. There by the rental car counter stood Mike—holding two dozen pink roses.

My heart skipped a beat and I felt faint.

244

"Mike?" Slowly, I walked to meet him, unsure of how to react. He looked like he had just stepped out of the pages of a magazine.

He hesitated a moment, then bent down and drew me into a hug, burying his face in my hair. "Jenny," he whispered. "I am so sorry. I was such an idiot—I never should have listened to my dad."

I pulled away from him and looked up into his green eyes. Why did he have such an effect on me? "I really don't know what to think. Why are you even here?" I flashed back to the hurt and anger of that day in the park.

He stepped back awkwardly. "Yeah, I kind of figured that out when you wouldn't answer my texts."

"You were a jerk."

"I know." He handed me the bouquet of roses. "We have a lot to talk about. Do you think your mom and dad would be okay with me driving you home?"

"Maybe." I looked over at my parents, who were eyeing Mike suspiciously. "I'm not so sure I *want* to talk to you right now."

I left Mike behind, and walked back to my parents. I gave them a pleading look. "Help me. I don't know what to do."

Dad looked over at Mike doubtfully. "I don't want him hurting you again."

Mom grabbed my hands and looked me in the eye. "Do you want to go with him?"

"I'm not sure," I answered truthfully.

She gave me a worried look. "It's up to you."

I was so confused. Maybe I would get closure if I talked to him. "Can you guys bring my bags home?"

"Sure." Dad gave me a hug and whispered in my ear. "If you have any trouble with him, you call me, okay?"

"I'm sure it will be fine."

I walked back to Mike. He put his arm around me. I bristled, and removed it.

"I hope someday you can forgive me." He looked almost defeated. "Look." He pulled something out of his pocket.

The little bentwood box that I had given him was sitting in the palm of his hand. He opened it and pulled out the moonstone heart. "I kept this with me every day you were gone."

I swallowed hard.

He put the heart and the box back in his pocket. Then he reached his hand out to me. I looked up at him. His face was sincere—there was remorse and hope there.

I paused, took a deep breath, and took his hand in mine.

THE END

About the Author

Martina Dalton writes young adult fiction and lives in the Pacific Northwest with her family. Born and raised in Alaska, she can nimbly catch a fish, dress for rain, and know what to do when encountering a grizzly bear. Now living in the Seattle area, she uses those same skills to navigate through rush-hour traffic.

When she's not writing, she hangs out here: https://www.facebook.com/AuthorMartinaDalton

Made in the USA
San Bernardino, CA
19 October 2014